"Let's talk about this marriage," Jack said.

"I think you pretty much covered that at the chapel," Donna said. " 'You may kiss the bride,' " she intoned, imitating Reverend Thistle. " 'Thanks, I'll pass.' "

Hell, Jack hadn't meant anything by that. But what was the point of kissing Donna to seal a marriage they both knew was a fraud? "Look, we're married. But if we play the part of a married couple for a few months, then quietly have a 'trial separation,' no one will think anything of it. In a couple more months, we can get a divorce. We'll both be free to do what we want to do…. And since we won't be sleeping together, there won't be any complications."

"Ah," Donna said. "A platonic marriage."

"Of course."

Well, she thought, the oldest living virgin in the world had just become the oldest living *married* virgin….

Dear Reader,

Hectic life? Too much to do, too little time? Well, Silhouette Desire provides you with the perfect emotional getaway with this month's moving stories of men and women finding love and passion. So relax, pick up a Desire novel and let yourself escape, with six wonderful, involving, totally absorbing romances.

Ultratalented author Mary Lynn Baxter kicks off November with her sultry Western style in *Slow Talkin' Texan*, the story of a MAN OF THE MONTH whose strong desires collide with an independent lady—she's silk to his denim, lace to his leather... and doing all she can to resist this *irresistible* tycoon. A small-town lawman who rescues a "lost" beauty might just find his own Christmas bride in Jennifer Greene's heartwarming *Her Holiday Secret*. Ladies, watch closely as a *Thirty-Day Fiancé* is transformed into a forever husband in Leanne Banks's third book in THE RULEBREAKERS miniseries.

Don't dare miss the intensity of an innocent wife trying to seduce her honor-bound husband in *The Oldest Living Married Virgin*, the latest in Maureen Child's spectacular miniseries THE BACHELOR BATTALION. And when a gorgeous ex-marine shows up at his old flame's ranch to round up the "wife who got away," he discovers a daughter he never knew in *The Re-Enlisted Groom* by Amy J. Fetzer. *The Forbidden Bride-to-Be* may be off-limits...but isn't that what makes the beautiful heroine in Kathryn Taylor's scandal-filled novel all the more tempting?

This November, Silhouette Desire is the place to live, love and lose yourself...to sensual romance. Enjoy!

Warm regards,

Joan Marlow Golan
Senior Editor, Silhouette Desire

Please address questions and book requests to:
Silhouette Reader Service
U.S.: 3010 Walden Ave., P.O. Box 1325, Buffalo, NY 14269
Canadian: P.O. Box 609, Fort Erie, Ont. L2A 5X3

THE OLDEST LIVING MARRIED VIRGIN

MAUREEN CHILD

SILHOUETTE *Desire*

Published by Silhouette Books

America's Publisher of Contemporary Romance

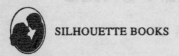

SILHOUETTE BOOKS

ISBN 0-373-76180-5

THE OLDEST LIVING MARRIED VIRGIN

Copyright © 1998 by Maureen Child

This edition published by arrangement with Harlequin Books S.A.

® and TM are trademarks of Harlequin Books S.A., used under license. Trademarks indicated with ® are registered in the United States Patent and Trademark Office, the Canadian Trade Marks Office and in other countries.

Printed in U.S.A.

MAUREEN CHILD

was born and raised in southern California and is the only person she knows who longs for an occasional change of season. She is delighted to be writing for Silhouette and is especially excited to be a part of the Desire line.

An avid reader, she looks forward to those rare rainy California days when she can curl up and sink into a good book. Or two. When she isn't busy writing, she and her husband of twenty-five years like to travel, leaving their two grown children in charge of the neurotic golden retriever who is the *real* head of the household. She is also an award-winning historical writer under the names Kathleen Kane and Ann Carberry.

To Jill Shalvis,
friend and fellow writer,
for long talks over cold plots,
shared laughter and huge
phone bills.
See you in Tahoe!

One

"**J**ust let me die," Donna Candello muttered as she rolled onto her right side, opened her eyes, then closed them. A helpless moan trickled from her throat.

Sunlight came pouring into the hotel room through floor-to-ceiling windows. Why hadn't she closed the drapes the night before? Good Lord, what a hideous thing to wake up to. Especially when her head was pounding with the mother of all hangovers.

Opening her eyes, she tried to get used to the golden light splashing across the industrial-gray carpet and the impersonal furniture. When her head didn't explode, she sighed and lifted one hand to push her black hair back from her face.

Lord, what a night.

From now on she would definitely eat something before trying to find courage at the bottom of a pitcher of margaritas. Heck, the only thing she'd eaten yesterday was the rock salt rimming her glass.

She made a face and licked dry lips with her thick, cottony tongue. Bracing both hands on the mattress, she pushed herself into a sitting position and watched as the world rocked, tilted, then thankfully righted itself.

Absently she noted the loud buzzing in her head and hoped it would wear off soon.

The blanket pooled at her waist and she glanced down to see she was still wearing her bra and panties. But then, the condition she'd been in last night, she was lucky she had remembered to take off her shoes before climbing into bed.

Heck, she had been lucky to find her room.

Suddenly a twinge of memory tugged at the corner of her mind, as persistent and nagging as the continued buzzing in her ears. Concentrating, Donna seemed to remember a very nice security guard in a dark blue uniform escorting her upstairs. Without his help, she probably never would have made it.

Too bad she couldn't remember his name or face. She owed him a big thank-you.

Abruptly the buzzing noise stopped. Before she could thank whatever gods were responsible, though, she heard the distinct sound of a man softly singing. And the sound was coming from behind the closed door of what she guessed was the bathroom.

Good Lord, that was no *buzz* she'd been hearing. It had been the shower.

Frantically, she tried to put a face to the voice of the man in the other room. But what was left of her brain drew a complete blank.

Dear Lord, she prayed silently, please don't let this be what it looked like. Please don't let her have been so drunk she'd slept with a man she couldn't even remember.

Briefly she cupped her face in her palms, trying to block out the man's voice. But she couldn't. Perfect, she said to herself, letting her hands fall to her lap. She'd gone from being the world's oldest living virgin to a one-night stand in one drunken night.

Well, she wasn't just going to sit here to wait for whoever he was to step out of the bathroom wearing nothing but a smile.

Casting a wary glance at the still-closed door, Donna edged clumsily off the bed and staggered to her feet. Spinning and swaying, the walls and furniture twisted and writhed like the characters in a Salvador Dali print.

Her stomach lurched and she clamped one hand over her mouth. Maybe it would be easier to just stay to face the no-good fink, she thought, then disregarded the notion entirely. She'd never had any experience with morning-after conversations before. And it wouldn't be fair to expect too much from herself while in the grips of a hangover.

Still, she briefly entertained the idea of jumping back into the bed and hiding under the covers. No, that wouldn't work.

She dropped to her knees beside the bed. Tossing her hair out of bloodshot eyes, she told herself to be calm. To think. To remember. Who was in her room? But it was no use. The night before was one long, foggy blank. Heck, she couldn't even remember registering at the hotel to *get* a room.

Donna inhaled sharply. Good God. If she didn't have a room, then *whose* room was she in?

Briefly she let her head drop to the rumpled sheets. Muttering into the mattress, she whispered, "What did you *do*, Donna? And *who* did you do it with?"

Abruptly the man in the bathroom stopped singing.

Donna looked up. She was trapped. Half-dressed, in a hotel where most of the guests were marines and their families, in town to celebrate the birthday of the Corps. Even if she made a break for the door, she was sure to run into people she knew. People her *father* knew. And some of those folks would be delighted to be able to spread gossip about Donna Candello running around half-dressed through one of the biggest hotels in Laughlin, Nevada.

She groaned at the thought and told herself there had to be a way to salvage this situation. If only her brain wasn't still hazy with lingering traces of too many margaritas.

How would she ever face her father?

How would she ever be able to look *herself* in the mirror again?

"Stupid, stupid, stupid," she moaned, slamming her forehead into the mattress to punctuate each word.

The doorknob turned.

Donna looked up, frantic. Black hair fell across her eyes. She squinted as the door opened slowly. The only thing missing, she thought, was the telltale horror movie music—to let the audience know that the dummy heroine was about to meet her maker.

The man in the open doorway didn't *look* like your typical villain. But hadn't she read somewhere that most serial killers looked like the boy next door?

In the next instant she realized that this guy didn't match *that* description, either. She reached up, pushed her hair out of her eyes and looked into a disapproving gray stare. Dressed only in a pair of faded blue jeans, his feet and chest bare, he looked perfectly at ease. Except for those eyes of his.

"So, you're finally awake," he said.

"Who are you?" Her voice sounded creaky.

"Jack Harris," he told her, flipping the hand towel he held across one shoulder. Then he crossed his arms over an incredibly wide, muscular chest and leaned negligently against the doorjamb. "Like I told you last night."

Harris. Harris, she repeated mentally. Why did that name sound familiar? She silently vowed to never again visit a friendly bartender as a therapist.

Trying to recover some of her dignity, which wasn't easy in her bra and panties, Donna stood, telling herself that she wore less clothing on the beach. There was no reason to feel self-conscious. Still, she folded her arms over her breasts, each hand gripping a bare shoulder.

Clearing her throat, she admitted, "I'm afraid I don't really remember much about last night."

He snorted.

Her eyebrows arched.

"Not surprising," he said tightly. "You could hardly stand up by the time I found you."

"Which was *when* exactly?" she asked, throwing dignity to the wind. She wanted to know what happened.

"About twenty-two thirty hours last night. Trying to get into the Battalion Ball through the emergency exit."

Oh, Lord.

"I stopped you just before the alarm could go off."

Dimly, she thought she recalled standing in the darkness, tugging and yanking at a door that had stubbornly refused to budge.

Oh, this just kept getting better.

Unconsciously, she lifted one hand from her shoulder to rub at an aching throb settling just between her eyebrows. "Look, Mr. Harris—"

"First Sergeant Harris," he amended.

First Sergeant Harris. Of course. *That's* how she knew the name. Not a serial killer. Worse.

A marine.

Donna stared at him, horrified at the implications of having spent the night in his room. No, surely she hadn't been drunk enough to— She cut that thought off at the pass, turned around and plunked onto the edge of the bed.

But wouldn't that be truly ironic? The last living twenty-eight-year-old virgin finally does the deed and is too drunk to remember it?

What an idiot she was!

Shaking her head carefully, Donna muttered more to herself than him. "I don't remember much from last night, First Sergeant."

"Like I said," he remarked, "I'm not surprised."

She ignored his sarcasm. She was in no shape to fire back. "I *do* remember a security guard bringing me here. But I don't remember *your* arrival."

Shaking his head, Jack Harris straightened, threw his towel back into the bathroom, then stalked across the room to a closet. Opening it up, he talked as he pulled out her dress and a pale green polo shirt for himself.

She frowned slightly. Where did all of the men's clothes come from?

"A security guard?" he asked, tossing a scooped-necked, floor-length, red velvet gown at her. "That's what you remember?"

"Yes," she snapped, grabbing the dress and holding it close to her body, luxuriating in the feel of something familiar. "And, I might add, he was decidedly more polite than you have been so far this morning.''

''That's wonderful,'' he muttered, and yanked his shirt over his head. She tried not to notice the play of muscles beneath his darkly tanned skin.

She was in enough trouble already. Besides, a great build didn't make up for a nasty manner. What did *he* have to be cranky about? *She* was the one with the hangover here. *She* was the one who had lost her virginity to a man who only seemed vaguely familiar.

She scowled to herself. Just what did it say about this guy, anyway? Did he usually lurk around hotels hoping to find a drunk woman he could take advantage of? Getting angrier by the minute, she realized he had probably felt as though he'd hit the jackpot when he'd discovered she was a virgin!

Lifting her chin, and holding her dress in front of her like a shield, she said quite calmly, ''I really think you should be going, Sergeant.''

''First Sergeant.''

Like that mattered *now*.

''Fine. First Sergeant. It's morning. You're dressed. Why don't you run along to your own room?''

He shoved the hem of his shirt into the waistband of his jeans. ''You're really something, you know that?''

''What a lovely thing to say,'' she said stiffly, then winced as a sharp pain darted across her forehead. Groaning slightly, she added, "Do all of your women curl up their toes and swoon at that line?"

"It wasn't a compliment."

"My mistake. I thought you were striving toward politeness."

"You expect 'polite' from a man who just spent the night sleeping on the floor because his bed was being used by a self-indulgent drunk?"

She jumped to her feet and knew immediately that it had been a mistake. Pain exploded behind her eyes. Her stomach pitched and Jack Harris seemed to fade in and out as her eyes desperately tried to focus.

Donna felt herself falling forward, but before she could hit the floor, he was there. Grabbing her, holding her close. The rock-hard strength of his chest seemed like the only stable point in her universe at the moment, so she held on as if it meant her life.

After a few terrifying seconds, it was over.

"Thank you," she murmured and, almost regretfully, pushed away from him.

He nodded, watching her carefully as if he half expected her to keel over again.

"I'm all right," she said.

One dark eyebrow lifted over his left eye.

"Wait a minute," Donna said, inhaling slowly, deeply. "You said *your* bed? Are you trying to tell me this is *your* room?"

"That's right."

"Then—" She took a halting step backward.

"Why would the security guard bring me here? To you?"

"That was no security guard, honey," he said. "That was me."

She stared at him. Bits and pieces of memory fluttered through her mind like autumn leaves in a whirlwind. Her gaze narrowed as she studied him, trying to fit his face with the half-remembered image of the guard who had been so kind.

Oh, Lord, she thought on an inward groan. He was right. It wasn't a dark blue security uniform she remembered. It was a Dress Blue uniform. Jack Harris had been formally dressed last night for the Battalion Ball.

Maybe they'd all be better off if she simply looked for an oven to stick her head into.

"This is mortifying," she finally mumbled. Drunk and rooming with a strange marine for the night. Waking up in only her underwear, in *his* bed, with no memory of how she got there.

Looking up at him, she forced herself to ask the fateful question. "Did we—" She jerked her head at the bed behind her. "You know..."

Jack felt his features tighten. Looking down into those deep brown eyes of hers, he clearly recalled having to strip off her gown and tuck her beneath the blankets. It hadn't been easy, turning his back on a gorgeous woman, even a drunk one. But, damn it, there were rules about some things. Whether he liked it or not. "No. We didn't 'you know....'"

Finding her drunk, trying to get into the ball, had

been pure chance. If he hadn't stepped outside for a cigarette, he never would have seen her. Dressed as she was and as determined as she had been to get into the party, he had known that she belonged with some poor marine. It had seemed like his duty to keep the clearly toasted woman from embarrassing herself, and the damn fool who loved her, in front of his superior officers.

He had taken her to his room with the thought of sobering her up. But she'd fallen asleep almost immediately. Now he had to find out where she belonged and get her there.

Fast.

"Nothing happened last night, lady," he said stiffly, turning his back on her to walk across the room and pick up his shirt.

"Oh."

He glanced at her unreadable expression and didn't know whether she was relieved or disappointed. Either way, though, it didn't matter a damn to him.

"Now, why don't you tell me who I should call about you?" he asked, determined to get her the hell out of his life as quickly as possible. *Before* the rest of the hotel guests woke up and someone saw her leaving his room.

"In case you hadn't noticed," she said, gingerly stepping into her red velvet dress, "I am no longer drunk, so I don't need you to phone anyone about me."

Disgusted, he told her, "Honey, this hotel is

crawling with marines. If you leave my room wearing last night's dress, somebody's going to notice and talk. Now, tell me who to call, so they can bring you something to wear.''

She fumbled with the tiny seed-pearl buttons lining her dress from the low-cut bodice to mid-thigh. He closed his eyes, not really wanting to look again at the high, wide slit in the front of her gown that exposed slim, shapely thighs. No reason why he should torture himself.

Man, this was the last time he'd be a Good Samaritan. Next time some gorgeous brunette was trying to embarrass herself, he'd let her.

Impatiently, Jack waited for her to answer him. Just before she finished her task, someone knocked on the door.

She looked up at him, her eyes wide.

"Damn it," he whispered. He had wanted to get this woman settled and out of his room before anyone else had a chance to see her. Quickly, Jack checked his watch—0930 hours. After last night, who in the heck would be up this early pounding on his door?

"Who is it?" she asked in a hush.

"How the hell should I know?" he snapped, then frowned. He felt like a cheating husband in an old movie. Well, that was nuts. He hadn't done anything wrong. He was the good guy here. All he'd tried to do was help a lady in distress.

But then, what was that old saying? *No good deed goes unpunished?*

The knocking sounded out again. Louder this time. Insistent.

Jack started for the door, but stopped dead when he heard the angry voice on the other side of it.

"First Sergeant Harris?"

"Colonel Candello?" Jack asked.

"Daddy?" Donna groaned.

"Daddy?" Jack repeated, horrified.

Two

Tearing his gaze from the woman in front of him, he shot a quick glance at the door before turning a malevolent glare on her again. "Colonel Candello is your *father?*"

"Yes," she whispered, frantically finger-combing her tousled hair. "How do I look?"

"Like hell," he muttered, and thought it appropriate since they were both standing in the middle of an inferno.

Damn it, why was the colonel here this early? Did the man already know about his daughter spending the night? And if he did, how? Jack hadn't thought even the marine wives could manage to spread gossip at light speed.

"First Sergeant Harris," the colonel said in a

tightly controlled voice, "are you going to keep me standing in the hall?"

Jack ran one hand across the top of his high and tight haircut and tried to think. His room was on the eleventh floor, so there was no sneaking her out the French doors that opened onto the balcony. And the room was too damned small to hide her for long. No choice here, he told himself.

Turning a hard stare on the colonel's daughter, he asked, "You ready to face the music?"

No.

Even without a mirror, Donna knew what she must look like. Standing there in her stocking feet, her dress wrinkled, smudged mascara shadowing her eyes... She groaned inwardly. No doubt she looked as if she'd spent a hot, passionate night with a wildly attentive lover.

How ironic.

She was about to be caught, tried, and convicted for something she hadn't done.

Had *never* done.

Good God, she hadn't seen her father in four years because she'd been too embarrassed to face him. After today, she'd have to move to Outer Mongolia.

Grimly, she nodded, threw her shoulders back and tried to look nonchalant.

Jack moved to the door, unlocked it, and opened it wide, silently inviting the colonel inside. "Good morning, Sir," he said as the man walked into the room.

"Is it?" the colonel asked.

Dressed in civilian clothes, Thomas Candello was still an imposing figure. In gray slacks and a pale blue, short-sleeved sport shirt, he looked younger than he did when in full uniform. But he was every inch as intimidating as usual.

Her father's gaze seemed to bore into Donna's and she flinched slightly at the disappointment she saw glittering in those brown eyes so like her own.

"Sir—" Jack started.

The colonel interrupted him. "Would you mind leaving my daughter and me alone for a few minutes, First Sergeant?"

Donna flicked a glance at her erstwhile host. She saw the hesitation on his features and knew that he desperately wanted to stay in the room to take his share of whatever the colonel had come to deliver. She also knew that he wouldn't think of disobeying even a nicely phrased "request" from her father.

"Aye, Sir," he said brusquely, and stepped into the hall, pulling the door closed behind him.

Donna wanted to run. But then, she'd run away four years ago and it hadn't done her any good. This time she'd stick it out. Amazing, she thought. Today, she had courage.

"Why didn't you tell me you were coming, Donna?"

She pushed her hair out of her eyes and wished to high heaven for three pots of hot, black coffee. How did everyone expect her to think when she had a hangover strong enough to kill a moose?

Inhaling sharply, she finally said, "I wanted to surprise you." Shrugging, she added helplessly, "Surprise!"

He didn't smile.

But she hadn't expected him to.

"Look, Daddy, this is all a big mistake," she said, moving away from the bed and all of its implications. "It's perfectly innocent, actually."

"'Innocent'?" He shook his head and she noticed absently that there were a few streaks of gray at his temples. "You spend the night with my First Sergeant, a man you've never met before, and you call it innocent?"

Why did she suddenly feel as though she were seventeen and late coming home from a date? She was twenty-eight years old. She'd been living on her own for years. She had a master's degree. As a sign language interpreter, her expertise was in demand everywhere from colleges to corporate battlegrounds.

Yet one look from her father had her dipping her head and mumbling answers.

"It's not what you think," she told him on a tired sigh. "The sergeant—"

"First sergeant," he cut in.

"Whatever." She waved one hand dismissively. "Jack was just trying to be helpful." Great. Now she'd been reduced to defending the man she'd wanted to kick only a few minutes ago.

But what choice did she have? The colonel was her father. The man wasn't going to stop loving her no matter how disappointed he was in her. He was also Jack Harris's commanding officer, and Jack didn't need to take career heat for her mistake.

The colonel walked over to the only chair in the room and sat. Leaning forward, his forearms on his thighs, he looked at her solemnly. "Do you know that at least four different people have already felt it was their 'duty' to come and tell me where my daughter spent the night?"

"Oh, Lord," she said on a sigh.

"Why, Donna?" he asked.

She walked to the French doors and opened them, bravely facing the sunshine just to breathe in the fresh, morning air. She stepped onto the narrow balcony and curled her fingers around the railing. "I had a couple of drinks at the airport when I landed."

"So, you were drunk, too."

She glanced at him and noted that a well-remembered muscle in his cheek was twitching. When she was a kid, that had always been her signal that she'd pushed him too far. Oh, not that he'd ever raised a hand to her. But Tom Candello's silence was as bad as any other man's rage.

"I guess the alcohol affected me more than usual because I forgot to eat," she said.

"And that makes it all right?"

"No, but that's what happened."

"And what's your reason for wanting a drink before seeing me?"

"Because I couldn't face you," she admitted, coming back into the room.

Planting both hands on his knees, he pushed himself to his feet. Towering over her by a good six or seven inches, he met her gaze and held it. ''Because I was right about Kyle? *That's* why you didn't want to face me?''

''Kyle's only a part of it and you know it,'' she said quickly, not wanting to get into a discussion about her ex-fiancé—or what had happened the last time she'd seen her father. ''As long as we're on the subject, it's not easy having a father who's always right.''

''Not always,'' he corrected, his mouth still a grim line of disapproval.

''Often enough to make me think my judgment stinks.'' And, to be honest, in the case of her ex-fiancé, it *had* stunk. Big time.

The colonel raised one dark eyebrow. ''Apparently, it still does.''

She mentally flinched at that one.

''We're straying from the point here, Donna.''

''What *is* the point, Dad?'' She was tired. And her head hurt. And her stomach felt as if there was an 8.1 earthquake rattling around inside it.

She needed a bath, some coffee and maybe, if it wouldn't kill her, a little food.

''The point is that half the battalion is already talking about you and First Sergeant Harris.'' He paused and frowned. ''The other half will be as soon as they hear about it.''

''I'm sorry,'' she said. ''I didn't mean to create such a mess.''

''Sorry doesn't cut it, Donna,'' he told her sternly.

"I don't know what you want me to do," she said, and pushed past him to sit in the chair he had vacated.

A quiet knock on the door interrupted whatever he would have said.

"Come in, First Sergeant," the colonel said. When the door opened, he added, "I'm sorry to have kept you out of your room so long."

"Not a problem, Sir," Jack said, closing the door quietly behind him. "But if you'll pardon me for saying so, Sir, there *is* a problem you should know about."

The colonel rubbed the back of his neck tiredly. "What is it?"

"Well, Sir…" Jack went on, clearly uncomfortable. "Major Collins's wife spoke to me in the hall just now."

"Great," the colonel muttered, and Donna flicked a quick, worried glance at him. "What'd she say?"

Jack came almost to attention. "Sir, she said she saw your daughter and me enter my room last night. She wanted to know when your daughter and I were getting married and why she wasn't invited."

"The old—" The colonel's voice trailed off into nothingness.

"Great," Donna muttered. "My sex life—" *Or lack of one,* she added silently "—is the talk of the marines." She shifted uneasily in the chair. If she had just stayed in Maryland, none of this would be happening. She would still have a perfectly good phone relationship with her father and she wouldn't be sitting in the first sergeant's room with him looking at her as if she were the Three Stooges and Mata Hari all in one.

"It'll blow over, Dad," she said tentatively, and was rewarded with a black look from her father.

"You know how gossip spreads," he said simply. "It gets bigger, not smaller."

All her fault, she thought, disgusted with herself.

"Sir." Jack spoke up again, and Donna and her father turned to look at him. "If I might make a suggestion?"

"First Sergeant," the colonel said wearily, "I could use a good one right about now."

"The only way to stop gossip is to make it less interesting," Jack said, still amazed that he was even considering saying what he was about to say. He glanced at the hungover woman mumbling to herself, then shifted his gaze back to her father.

The man he owed so much to.

"Your point, First Sergeant?"

"My point is this, Sir." He sucked in a gulp of air and said the rest of it in a rush, before he could change his mind. "If you agree, your daughter and I can get married this afternoon. If we're married, the gossips will have nothing to talk about."

"*Excuse* me?" Donna jumped up from her chair, wobbled a bit, then grabbed her father's arm for support. Jack only glanced at her before looking back at the colonel.

"We can tell people we got married last night. No one would have to know any different."

The other man was silent for a long, thoughtful minute.

Jack looked at the officer across the room from him. He had admired and respected Colonel Candello for years. Standing out in the hall, with nothing to do but think, Jack had realized that because of his actions, the colonel's reputation would be sullied.

It was then he'd come up with his plan. Sure, it was a sacrifice. But there was nothing Jack wouldn't do for the colonel.

"That's quite a suggestion, First Sergeant," the officer said.

"It's nuts, is what it is." Donna spoke up, but neither man was listening at the moment.

"We can drive to Vegas," Jack continued, ignoring her for the moment. "It's only an hour away. We'll find an out-of-the-way chapel, take care of business and be back here before most of the battalion is even awake."

"It might work," the colonel said.

"Maybe," Donna agreed, nodding her head at the two of them. "Except for one little detail."

"Ma'am?" Jack asked, only to be polite.

"What detail is that, darling?" the colonel asked.

"The fact that I'm *not* going to go through with it," Donna told them.

Her father's features tightened a bit. Jack saw it from across the room. As the Candellos faced each other, he waited silently. He'd seen the colonel in action and he didn't have a doubt as to who would win this silent competition.

"Daddy," she said so softly Jack almost couldn't hear her. "You can't be serious."

"Why not, honey?" he asked, reaching out and laying both hands on her shoulders.

"For one thing, I don't even know him."

"That didn't stop you last night."

Jack tensed.

"I *told* you, nothing happened," Donna insisted.

"No one will believe that," her father said.

True enough, Jack thought. No doubt the major's wife was already spreading her story from one end of Laughlin to the other.

"But, Dad, this is practically medieval."

"I can't force you to do anything," the colonel said, his hands still gripping his daughter's shoulders.

"I can't marry a stranger, for God's sake," she whined.

Jack hated whiny women.

"He's not a stranger," the colonel insisted. "I've known First Sergeant Harris over fifteen years."

She shot Harris a glare through mascara-smudged eyes, then looked back at her father. "Then *you* marry him."

"Donna..."

"No way." She shook her head.

"What was it you were just saying about your judgment?" the colonel asked.

"That was different."

"How?"

Jack frowned slightly. He didn't have a clue what they were talking about now.

"Do you trust me?" the colonel asked quietly.

"Of course," she answered. "This has nothing to do with trust, though."

The colonel's hands dropped from her shoulders. He stood for a long, quiet minute, staring into her eyes.

Jack had the distinct feeling that there was a silent message being passed from father to daughter. But he was in no position to know what it was.

"Well, then," the colonel said softly. "If you won't, you won't. But I *am* disappointed, Donna."

Three

"I do," Donna said, and extended her left ring finger toward her new husband. The thin gold band felt surprisingly heavy on her hand.

Shortest wedding ceremony on record, she thought numbly. Assembly line marriages, no waiting. The preacher kept talking, though to Donna, his words sounded like little more than a low hum of sound. She couldn't believe she was actually doing this. Maybe she wasn't, she thought desperately. Maybe this was all just a really bad dream.

"I do," Jack said from beside her. His voice rumbled along her spine, letting her know that this was no dream.

The Reverend Thistle, a man whose frowsy white hair and long, sticklike body made him strangely resemble the weed he was named for, quietly closed his worn, leather Bible and said, "I now pronounce you husband and wife." He beamed benevolently at First Sergeant Harris. "You may kiss the bride."

Donna looked up into his cold, expressionless eyes and wasn't the slightest bit surprised to hear him say, "Thanks, I'll pass."

Forcing a smile for the perplexed reverend, Donna made her way back up the aisle toward the puddle of sunshine outside. *Go toward the light,* she thought grimly. Except for her, when she reached that bright light, there would be no salvation. Just a short car ride back to the hotel in Laughlin, where her father waited.

She glanced down at the ring on her finger again. There hadn't been time to locate a jewelry store. The simple gold band had come straight from the Reverend Thistle's collection of wedding rings for unprepared couples.

Twenty-five dollars' worth of gold plating, a silk flower bouquet, and the only witnesses to her wedding, the next couple in line.

Tears stung her eyes, but she blinked them back determinedly. Her own father hadn't given her away. Her bottom lip quivered and she bit down on it hard. He had already scheduled a golf game with the general. If he'd broken the date, he would have needed to explain. And explanations were one of the things they were trying to avoid.

Donna stepped into the bright Vegas sun and immediately shielded her eyes with her hand. Even in

November, the desert produced sunshine like nowhere else.

Rummaging one-handed in her purse, she looked
for her sunglasses while waiting for Jack to come out
of the chapel. When she found them, she slipped
them on, grateful for the dark lenses. Turning around,
she glanced at the front of the Chapel of the Desert.
Palm trees, fake brick and a do-it-yourself stained-
glass window above the front doors.

Well, this was a far cry from the wedding she had
planned so meticulously four years ago. Then, she
had reserved the church months ahead of time. She'd
had six bridesmaids, two flower girls and a ring
bearer. Not to mention a groom who had actually
professed to love her.

She scowled slightly at that last thought. All right,
so it hadn't been perfect.

"Are you okay?" Jack asked as he stepped out of
the chapel to join her on the walk.

"Peachy," she muttered darkly.

"Yeah," he said, shifting his gaze to stare at the
crowds of gamblers already clogging the city side-
walks in their hot pursuit of instant riches. "It's been
a helluva day so far, huh?"

He was still wearing the pale green polo shirt and
faded jeans he'd put on a couple of hours ago. Hardly
formal wear. But then, her simple blue cotton skirt
and matching, short-sleeved sweater was hardly a
cover picture for a bridal magazine.

He pulled sunglasses out of his shirt pocket and

stared at her from behind the safety of darkness. "You ready to head back?"

"What?" she asked, and couldn't seem to stop the sarcasm dripping off her tongue. "No reception?"

One corner of his mouth lifted, then fell again. "Oh, we'll get a reception," he told her. "I'm just not sure what kind."

Ah, the perfect end to the perfect wedding, she thought, and grimly started after him as he headed for the car.

Under the shade of an umbrella table on the deck overlooking the Colorado River, Jack took a good long look at his new wife.

Wife.

He just managed to hide a shudder.

Even though this had been his idea, he still had a hard time dealing with the fact that he was actually married. To the colonel's daughter, no less.

Not that marrying into an officer's family would get him anywhere careerwise. The U.S. Marine Corps was probably the last bastion of antinepotism in the free world. If anything, he'd probably be the butt of all kinds of jokes from his friends.

Still, the deed was done now, and they'd just have to live with it. At least for a while. And that was what he wanted to talk to the "little woman" about.

"This doesn't have to be hard," he said firmly, noticing that she winced at the tone of his voice.

Rubbing her forehead with her fingertips, she said, "Do you have to speak so loudly?"

"Still feeling the effects of that hangover?" he asked unnecessarily. Lord, he'd never seen a woman less suited to drinking. He'd be willing to bet that there were people on their deathbeds feeling better than she was right at the moment.

"Yes," she muttered. "Is there any more coffee?"

He picked up the beige carafe from the center of the table and shook it. Nothing. "You drank it all."

"Get more," she said desperately. *"Please."*

"No problem." He looked up, caught the waitress's eye and hefted the carafe. She nodded. Turning back to his blushing bride, he said, "It's coming."

"Thank God." She pushed her uneaten lunch away from her, set her elbows on the glass-topped table and cupped her face in her hands.

Jack shook his head, leaned back in his chair and stretched his legs out in front of him, crossing them at the ankle. "You're a lousy drunk," he commented dryly.

She lifted her head long enough to glare at him. "I probably just need practice."

"Don't do this often?" he asked. Maybe it was a personal question. But they were married now, and he wanted to know if he'd saddled himself with a lush.

Her voice muffled by her palms, she asked, "Why would anyone want to do this *often?*"

That had always been his point of view, too. But there were plenty of folks more than willing to suffer the pain for the few hours of a pleasant buzz.

"I can't figure out that one myself," he said, keeping his voice low enough to not be painful to her. "But lots of people do. What I want to know is, are you one of them?"

Their waitress arrived, picked up the empty carafe and set a replenished one in its place. Donna sat up, reached for it, and poured herself what had to be her tenth cup of coffee.

Cupping the mug between her palms, she looked at her new husband over the rim, inhaled the rich steam and said plainly, "No, First Sergeant. I don't drink." She took a sip, shuddered and qualified that statement by adding, "Usually."

"Glad to hear it," he told her. "You don't seem to have a talent for it."

"Now *there's* an understatement."

He caught himself before he could actually smile. Damn it, he didn't want to like her. He didn't want to feel anything for her.

"I think we should get a few things straight," he said.

"Shoot," she muttered. "Please."

Jack swallowed another reluctant smile. "See, I didn't plan on marrying you."

She snorted. "Well, *duh.*"

He studied her for a long minute. "Are you always this sarcastic?"

"Always," she said after another sip. "But it's a lot pithier when I'm in pain."

"I'll keep that in mind."

"Probably safer."

Jack helplessly shook his head in admiration.

Damn, he was going to have an uphill battle not getting real fond of her. Her chin-length black hair twisted in the breeze off the river. She wasn't wearing her sunglasses, so he got a good look at those brown eyes he'd noticed right away last night. Even blurred by the glassy haze of alcohol, they'd been remarkable. Now, offset as they were by the blood-shot whites of her eyes, the liquid chocolate brown seemed to shimmer with depths he didn't even want to consider. Delicate, black brows arched high on her forehead and her full lips were tight with the pain throbbing in her head.

Damn, she looked good.

"How old are you?" he asked suddenly.

One of those delicate brows lifted high over her right eye. "Awfully personal for our first date, don't you think?"

"Since our first date was also our wedding, no, I don't think so."

"Hmm," she said. "Point taken. All right, I'm twenty-eight."

His brain raced for a minute. "But the colonel's only forty-five."

She smiled and gave him a wink that quickly became a wince. "That's right. He really prefers it if people don't do the math."

"But that would have made him only—"

"Seventeen when I was born."

Jack whistled, low and long.

"Before you ask," she went on, her voice tight, "Mom was sixteen. Though the older I got, the younger my mother used to get, so it's hard to be sure.''

"Must have been hard on them," he said more to himself than to her.

"I'm sure it was," she told him. "But selfishly speaking, I can't really be sorry, can I?"

"Suppose not."

"So," she said, pulling in a deep breath. "You said you wanted to talk about something. I'm guessing it's not about my parents and their rather embarrassing history."

"No, it's not." He cocked his head to look at her carefully. "You sure you're up to this right now?"

"Probably not," she admitted. "But this is as good as it's going to get for several hours."

"Okay…" He hesitated, suddenly unsure of just how to put this. "We got married for your father's reputation's sake, right?"

"Do we have to go there again?"

"No. What I want to talk about is the future, not what already happened."

"What future?"

"Ours," he said. "This marriage."

"Well," she said as she leaned back cautiously in her chair, "I think you pretty much covered that back at the chapel."

"What?" Maybe she wasn't feeling up to this conversation.

"'You may kiss the bride,'" she intoned in a pretty good imitation of Reverend Thistle. "'Thanks,'" she mocked pointedly. "'I'll pass.'"

Now it was his turn to wince. Hell, he hadn't meant anything by that. But what would have been the point of kissing her to seal a marriage they both knew was a fraud?

"What'd you expect?" he asked.

"Orange blossoms, organ music, crowds of people, my *father,*" she said with a sniff.

Jack tensed. Here he'd been ready to like her and now she was going to cry on him.

"Let's not make this something it isn't," he said quickly, relieved when he saw her blink away the moisture in her eyes.

"Don't worry, Sergeant—"

"First Ser—"

"I know." She cut him off. "Look, I didn't want this any more than you did, okay? You're safe. I'm not going to become the little wifey and follow you around the base like a lost puppy."

"That's what I want to talk about," he said. "Just exactly what we both expect from this marriage."

She lifted one hand to rub her temple. When she didn't speak, Jack continued.

"We're married," he said, sitting up and leaning toward her. "But it doesn't have to stay that way."

Her hand dropped to her lap. She looked at him thoughtfully. "Go on," she prompted.

"If we play the part of a married couple for a few months, then quietly have a trial separation, no one will think anything of it."

"'Trial separation'?" she repeated.

"Sure. Then after a couple more months, we get

a divorce. We're both free to do what we want to do."

"A divorce." She managed to keep from shuddering. He made it all sound so cut and dried. But it wasn't. At least not to her. Donna had always thought that once she was married, she'd *stay* married. But then, she'd always dreamed that she'd marry for love, too.

"You have a problem with that?"

"Call me dysfunctional," she said with a shrug she hoped would hide the dismay rushing through her. "My parents' divorce was a nightmare. I was only two years old, but I grew up listening to my mother complain about my father. I didn't even really get to know him until I was almost thirteen."

"That's different," Jack said. He was sorry to hear about the colonel's troubles, but that kind of thing wouldn't affect Donna and him. If he was honest, he wasn't a big supporter of easy divorces and broken marriages either. But then, this wasn't a real marriage, was it? "We won't have kids to worry about upsetting."

"Not in three months," she assured him. "I'm good, but even Super Woman would require at least nine."

He sighed heavily. "I *meant* that we wouldn't be sleeping together, so there wouldn't be any complications."

"Ah," Donna said, carefully nodding as if her head was about to fall off. "A platonic marriage."

"Of course," he said. Crossing his arms over his

chest, he looked at her as if he was waiting for her to applaud.

Well, isn't this a wonderful turn of events? she thought.

The oldest living virgin in the world had just become the oldest living *married* virgin.

Four

She forced another swallow of coffee down her throat. Why did things like this keep happening to her? She wasn't a bad person. She didn't go out of her way to hurt people. Heck, she even hated calling an exterminator to wipe out bug civilizations.

And still she managed to screw up her life on a regular basis.

Risking a still-bleary-eyed glance at her new husband, she could almost see what he was thinking. And it wasn't flattering.

"Fine, First Sergeant Harris," she said softly. "Platonic, it is. Your virtue is safe with me."

One corner of his mouth tilted up slightly, then flattened out again. He'd done that move several times already that morning. Either she amused him greatly or he had a serious facial tic. It must be the latter, she thought. What he could find entertaining about a sexless marriage between strangers was completely beyond her.

Then that tic flickered again.

"What's so funny?" she asked, despite the fact that his half smile was now gone.

"Trust me, Princess," he said. "I don't think there's *anything* funny in all this."

"Then why'd you do it?"

"Do it?"

"Marry me."

His long fingers curled through the handle of his coffee cup. "For your father."

"I figured that much out for myself," she said, suddenly exhausted with the morning's activities. Getting married could really take a toll on a person.

He nodded. "Let's just say I owe the man."

"Enough to marry his daughter?" One eyebrow lifted. "Must be quite a debt."

"I think so."

Intrigued, and more curious than she cared to admit, even to herself, she stared at him for a long moment before asking, "I don't suppose you'd care to share that information with me?"

Again that corner of his mouth tilted up briefly. "No, I wouldn't."

She tried a shrug and was immensely grateful when her head didn't roll off her shoulders.

"How about you?" he asked.

"What about me?"

"Why'd *you* agree to the wedding?"

Now there was a loaded question. One she wasn't prepared to discuss with a man she hardly knew, even if he *was* her husband. Old embarrassing memories rose up in her mind and she deliberately pushed them all to the back of her still-foggy brain.

"Let's just say *I* owed him, too."

"No sharing?"

A distinct twinkle shone at her from his gray eyes. The first sergeant? Teasing? "I think I'll pass," she said, not even realizing that she was throwing his earlier words back at him. The twinkle dissolved in a heartbeat.

"Look, Donna," he said, "for better or worse, we're married."

"For richer or poorer," she intoned solemnly. "In sickness and in health—"

"At least for now," he interrupted. "We may as well try to get along."

A romantic speech designed to bring flutters of happiness to any girl's heart, she muttered to herself as she rubbed at that spot between her eyes again, hoping to ease the throbbing ache. Nothing.

Squinting at him, she felt her stomach drop, as it did every time she rode a roller coaster. Ridiculous for a man's face to have that effect on her. Especially when it wasn't even a classically *handsome* face. Jack Harris was far too rugged and honed-looking to be called handsome. Attractive, sure, she supposed, in a rough-and-tumble sort of way. Her stomach pitched again and this time she ignored it.

He *did* have a point.

For the next few months at least, they would be married. Living together. So they wouldn't be sleeping together. Was that really so important?

Once again, she was on the roller coaster. The hangover, she told herself. It was just the hangover.

All right, they wouldn't be lovers. They would be *friends*. Or if not friends, noncombative opponents.

Good Lord, she sounded as marine-oriented as her new husband.

Taking a deep, steadying breath in the hopes of jumping off that stomach-lurching ride, she said, "Okay, First Sergeant—"

"Jack," he interrupted. "Call me Jack."

She nodded slowly. "Jack it is." Inhaling sharply, she sucked in the still cool air off the river before extending her hand in a gesture of peace. As he took her hand in his and shook it, she heard herself ask, "So, husband, do you snore?"

That night at dinner, Jack looked across the table at his wife and told himself to remember that this was, for all intents and purposes, a *pretend* marriage. But it wasn't easy.

She looked gorgeous. Amazing what the lack of a hangover could do for a woman. She wore a short, sunshine-yellow dress that hugged her curves, defining her many assets to perfection. The color of the dress deepened a honey-colored tan and somehow shifted the brown of her eyes to a shade of gold that drew his attention over and over again.

Sitting at the colonel's table was nerve-racking for Jack, but his new wife was completely at home. Of course, why wouldn't she be? Colonel Candello was her father. Raised by an officer, around officers, she actually *belonged* at that table.

As for him, Jack kept waiting for someone to leap up, point at him and shout. "This man's an imposter. He's not one of us. Get him out of here!" He grimaced slightly and told himself that the night was almost over. All he had to do was survive dessert. After that, he could go to his room and— Wait a minute. Not *his* room any longer. Now he shared it with a wife.

Mental images raced through his mind. Donna, tossing her newly purchased clothes and the bags they'd come in all over his hotel room. There had been no way to avoid her staying with him. A newly married couple wouldn't very well have separate rooms, after all.

So there wouldn't be any relaxation for him after dinner, either. Perfect. Why in the hell hadn't he just let her embarrass herself and the colonel the night before? Would it really have been so bad if the colonel's daughter had turned up drunk at the Battalion Ball?

Yeah, he thought. It would have. At least for the colonel.

"Jack?" that man asked in a tone of voice that clearly said he'd asked before and been ignored.

"Sir," Jack responded, unconsciously stiffening in

his seat. "Sorry, Sir, daydreaming, I guess." Or, to be more accurate, nightmaring.

"Relax, Jack," his new father-in-law said, "you're not on parade, here. This is just an informal, family dinner."

Family. Him? And the colonel? Lord help him.

"Of course, Sir," he said, no more at ease than he had been a moment ago.

The colonel shook his head, but asked out of the blue, "Do you play any golf?"

Golf? Jack stared for a long minute at the man he most admired in the world, thinking how little they really had in common. Where *he'd* grown up, there were no golf courses. That game was for rich people. People with too much time and money on their hands. The folks in Jack's neighborhood had been too busy trying to find work and buy food to go out and chase some little white ball around a well-tended lawn. But he couldn't very well voice that opinion to his superior officer, so he said only, "No, Sir, I don't."

"Too bad," the colonel said. "I think you'd like it. Donna's pretty good, you know."

Now why didn't that surprise him? His gaze shifted back to the pretty woman across from him. Of course the spoiled, only child of an important man would play golf. "Really?"

"I haven't played in years," Donna admitted. The first sentence she'd uttered since sitting at the table an hour ago.

"Maybe you could teach Jack," her father said.

"That's probably not a bad idea," she conceded with a quick look at her husband.

Her gaze barely rested on him an instant before she pointedly looked away again. So much for their hastily made bargain to try to be friendly. Hell, now that she was stone-cold sober, maybe she was regretting their quickie marriage.

Now *that* he could understand.

Damn, this was going to be harder than he'd thought, Jack told himself. He let his own gaze wander the crowded restaurant. He recognized several of the other diners as marines and even caught a couple of them throwing curious looks his way.

He shifted uncomfortably in his chair. Jack never had liked being the center of attention in any situation. Being a marine fed into that nicely. On base, he was simply one of thousands of soldiers. Now, though, he'd managed to step into the limelight, and he didn't care for it one bit.

"Would you two excuse me?" the colonel asked.

Jack turned to look at the other man. But the colonel's gaze was riveted on a spot at the far side of the room. As the older man pushed away from the table, he said, "I see someone I'd like a moment with."

He was gone before either of them could say a word.

"Well," Donna muttered as she followed her father's progress across the room. "I wonder what that's all about?"

"I don't know," Jack said, "but it's none of my business, either."

Both of her finely arched eyebrows lifted as she turned those brown eyes on him. "Feeling a little cranky, are we?"

"Cranky?" Stunned, he stared at her for a long minute. "*I'm* not the one who hasn't said a damn thing all night."

She winced. "Okay, so I haven't exactly been holding up my end of the conversation."

"You don't even *have* an end."

Those incredible golden eyes of hers narrowed slightly. "You know, I don't much like pushy husbands."

Amazing. He'd almost found himself liking her earlier. Wouldn't you know his new wife would be at her *most* likable when she had been suffering from a hangover?

"And I don't much like whiny wives."

"Whiny?" She sat straighter in her chair. "Who's whining? You just said yourself that I haven't even been talking."

"You can whine by intent, too."

"How do you know what I intended or not?"

"I can tell what you're thinking just by looking at your face."

"Oo-oh, a mind reader. How fascinating."

"Knock it off, Donna."

"Knock what off exactly, Jack?" she asked, leaning one elbow on the table. Cupping her chin in her hand, she batted her eyelashes at him wildly. "I thought you wanted me to talk."

Disgusted with himself, her, and the whole

damned situation, he snapped, "Forget it. I changed my mind."

"How like a man. Never sure what he wants."

"What's that supposed to mean?"

The humorous glint in her eyes was gone. "Never mind."

"Well, well," a booming deep voice announced from nearby, startling both of them into turning their heads toward the man just stopping at their table.

Immediately Jack jumped to his feet and came to attention. "General Stratton, Sir. Good evening."

The older man, dressed in a dove-gray suit, carried himself as if wearing a full dress uniform. "As you were, First Sergeant."

Jack relaxed only slightly, shifting into an "at ease" stance, arms behind his back.

"How's my favorite goddaughter and her new husband tonight?" the general asked, smiling down at Donna.

She stood slowly and rose up to kiss the older man on the cheek. "We're fine, Uncle Harry," she said.

General Stratton? Beads of sweat broke out on Jack's forehead. Uncle Harry? Good God, what had he gotten himself into here? By trying to save his colonel's reputation, he'd jumped headfirst into a pool he had no business trying to swim in. Generals. Colonels. Hell, he was drowning already and he hadn't been in the water for a whole day yet.

"You two should have waited," the general was saying as Jack focused on the conversation. "Had a big wedding on base, where we could all have been there."

Jack's mouth was very dry. He looked at his wife and in stupefied amazement, watched her smile at him as though she meant it before turning back to the general.

"Oh, Uncle Harry," she practically sighed, "it was so much more romantic this way."

Romantic? Memories of their less than perfect wedding flashed across his mind and Jack didn't know whether to be relieved or worried that his wife seemed to be such a good liar.

General Stratton bent, kissed her forehead, then straightened. "I suppose I can remember what young love is like," he said with a slow shake of his head. "Vaguely." Turning to face Jack, the general went on sternly. "You treat our girl right now, First Sergeant, or you'll answer to me."

Perfect.

"Yes, Sir," Jack said, his voice as stiff as his body.

Nodding, the older man gave Donna's shoulder a pat, then said, "You two enjoy yourselves. I've got to go find my wife before some young major runs off with her." His gaze already scanning the crowded dining room, he wandered away.

Jack and Donna, still standing at opposite ends of the table, stared at each other for a long minute. "Uncle Harry?" he asked.

She shrugged.

"Oh, man," he whispered, his rigid stance slumping a bit now that the general had moved on.

"What happened to the stalwart marine who rode so bravely to the rescue this morning when facing my dragon father?" she asked quietly.

"He's in shock." Along with what friends of his had already heard about his hurried marriage. Only a few more people to tell, he thought, not looking forward to seeing their astonished faces or hearing the gasps of "Donna who?"

"Maybe he needs a little exercise."

"Huh?" Jack looked at her blankly.

She shook her head and he tried not to notice how her soft, black hair caressed her cheeks with the movement.

"Dance with me, First Sergeant."

He gave the crowded dance floor a wary glance. Already, the small band was shifting into a slow song and couples were beginning to sway in time with the beat.

Donna came around the table and stood right in front of him. Cocking her head to one side, she looked up into his eyes. "Dance? You know, moving around a floor while music plays?"

"I know what it is," he told her, and didn't add that he usually avoided dance floors at all costs.

"Well, good," she said, and took his hand before he could object. Threading her way through the hundreds of small tables scattered around the room, she pulled him along in her wake.

Once among the other couples, she turned and

stepped into his arms. Automatically, Jack held her, his right arm sliding around her narrow waist, his left hand cupping her right. She smiled up at him and something hot and heavy settled in the pit of Jack's stomach.

He ignored the curious glances from the other dancers and stared into her eyes. Shadow and light played in their depths, captivating him. Her breasts pressed against his chest and he fancied that he could feel her heart beating in time with his own. His body stirred, responding to the warm nearness of her. He inhaled the soft, floral scent of her perfume and felt it slip into his soul.

"Jack?" she whispered.

"Hmm?" His right hand splayed open on her back, as if trying to hold more of her—*all* of her.

"Are you okay?"

"Yeah," he said, his gaze moving over her features as if he was seeing her for the first time.

"You're sure?"

One corner of his mouth tilted. "Why?"

She glanced from side to side, then back up into his eyes. Smiling, she answered him. "Because we're in the middle of the dance floor, standing still."

"I don't dance."

Shaking her head, she said, "Well, now's a fine time to tell me."

Another couple swung past them, bumping into Jack's back. He tightened his grip on her reflexively.

Her hips came into contact with his. No doubt she felt his body's reaction, since her eyes widened.

"Maybe we should go back to the table," she said.

"Nope." Maybe he was just plain nuts, Jack thought. But for the moment, all he wanted to do was continue to hold her. "You can teach me to dance. Now."

"Now?" she echoed. "Here?"

"Here."

After a momentary pause, she smiled again. "It's been a day of firsts, huh? Married in the morning, dancing lessons in the evening..." Her voice trailed off.

"And we still have the whole night ahead of us," Jack told her. "Who knows what *other* firsts are in store for us?"

Her eyes got even bigger and if he hadn't known better, Jack might have thought that Donna Candello Harris was worried about something. Maybe even...*scared*.

Five

This is no roller coaster, she thought wildly. This is the *grandfather* of all roller coasters. Her heartbeat skittered into overdrive and her hand trembled in his. Donna stared up into his gray eyes and watched each of their fine resolutions about a platonic marriage shatter.

Tiny sparks of electricity shimmered throughout her body. Her limbs felt as heavy and tingly as if she'd been asleep for years and was just now waking up. As that thought raced across her mind, Donna inhaled sharply, tugged her hand free of Jack's, and took a step backward.

"Donna?" His voice just carried to her over the sound of the band. "What's wrong?"

"This," she whispered, knowing he couldn't hear

her. Knowing, too, that she had to keep her distance from him. It would go away, she told herself firmly. This odd, heated response to his slightest touch. This was only the first day of their marriage. Surely in another week or two, she would be used to him. Probably sick and tired of him.

With any luck.

"Donna?" he asked again, moving in closer. "Are you all right?"

"No," she said, loud enough to be heard. "I'm pretty tired, Jack. I think I'll go up to the room."

His features tightened. His gray eyes cooled until they were the color of an ocean fog—and they held just as much warmth.

He cupped her elbow with one hand. "All right, I'll see you to the room."

Tingles. Sparks of heat. Desire sputtering into life.

Donna gulped in air and jerked free of his hold. "No need," she said haltingly as she tried to steady her racing heartbeat. "You stay. Have fun. I'll be fine."

Without giving him a chance to argue, she hurried off the dance floor. She paused only long enough to snatch up her handbag from the table before running for the exit as though he was chasing her.

She needn't have bothered.

Jack stood where she'd left him. Alone in a crowd of smiling couples.

The room was dark and quiet when Jack let himself in a couple of hours later. Exhausted, he told himself that maybe it hadn't been such a great idea to walk up and down the river boardwalk for two hours. But he hadn't been ready to face his new bride until now. He'd needed to cool off. Time for some quiet thinking. An hour or two to himself, where he could make up ridiculous reasons to excuse the rush of need that had filled him the moment Donna Candello had stepped into his arms.

And he'd come up with some beauties. Everything from overtiredness to uncontrollable chemistry with a gorgeous woman. Hell, it wasn't the first time he'd been attracted to someone he hardly knew. He was a man. Human. He was turned on by a knockout female just like any other guy.

But all of his reasoning fell flat. He knew it. He just didn't want to admit it. Because at no other time in his entire life had he felt so completely...*alive* as he had when he'd held Donna on that crowded dance floor. Just the memory of those few seconds was enough to send blood rushing to an area of his body that had already plagued him enough for one evening.

He stepped into the shrouded darkness and quietly closed and locked the door behind him. Toeing off his shoes, he pushed them up against the wall, out of the way. In the blackness, he couldn't see a thing, but he turned his head in the direction of the bed, knowing she was there. So close and yet so completely out of reach.

If he closed his eyes, he could still see her expression as she'd backed away from him earlier. She had looked horrified. Confused. Worried. He blinked away the image in favor of a more preferable one.

He saw her as he had the night before. Sprawled across his sheets, her black hair gleaming against the white pillowcase. Only, in his mind, she was sober. And waiting for him. She looked up at him, lifted her arms and smiled softly.

Jack took one instinctive step forward and the darkness exploded into a starburst of pain. He allowed one surprised grunt to escape his throat before clamping his lips tightly together. There was no need to frighten her out of a sound sleep just because he'd just broken his foot.

Bending, he grabbed the toe he had just slammed into something and rubbed it until the throbbing eased somewhat.

What the hell had he kicked? he wondered absently. As his eyes slowly became more accustomed to the darkness, shadows began to take shape. He noted the lighter rectangle on the wall that was the draperies, closed against the neon glitter of the night sky. He swiveled his head toward the bed again, but this time he saw plainly that Donna wasn't there.

Standing straight, he turned back toward whatever had almost crippled him. "What the hell?" he muttered. The two easy chairs in the room had been pulled close together, their seats matched up to form a small, uncomfortable-looking bed.

And on that makeshift bed, the quilt tucked up to her chin and the pillow stuffed against a chair armrest, his blushing bride lay sound asleep.

In the dim, shadowy light, he studied her calm, peaceful features. He heard the soft whisper of her even breathing. She whimpered slightly, then scooted around, apparently looking for a more comfy position, before nestling her head deeper into the pillow.

Unexpected anger simmered in his gut.

Why hadn't she slept in the damn bed? What was this supposed to be proving? That she couldn't bear to be in the same bed with him? Hell, it was a wonder she hadn't set up camp in the hallway!

"And how can she sleep through me slamming my foot into her blasted bed and shouting about it afterward?" he asked out loud, hoping for a response from Sleeping Beauty.

Nothing.

Disgusted, he turned toward the bathroom, took a step and then stopped, swiveling his head back to look at the still-oblivious woman.

She was *humming* in her sleep.

Jack scowled.

Not only was she humming, he thought furiously. She was off-key.

Twenty minutes later he stretched out on the floor, still damp from his shower. Dragging a sheet over him, he stuffed a pillow behind his head and glared at Donna. He would be damned if *he* would sleep in that bed while *she* slept on a chair.

Then, grabbing up a third pillow, he pulled it down over his face and ears, trying, without success, to drown out the blasted humming.

* * *

Two days later, back at the base, things weren't running any more smoothly.

Donna gripped the receiver tightly and tried to keep her voice even. She'd learned long ago that in dealing with people, it never paid to lose your temper.

"Excuse me, Lieutenant Austin," she interrupted the man's apparently well-rehearsed speech. "You're saying that there *is* base housing available, but we can't have it?"

"Yes, ma'am," he said, approval in his tone. "That's it exactly."

Donna sank back into her father's burgundy leather desk chair. "Then what you're really saying is, nothing's available."

"No, ma'am." The faceless lieutenant sighed, clearly disappointed in her. "We have a house for you and the first sergeant, but you can't have it for a day or two."

"And why is that again?"

"Like I told you before, ma'am," he said, "the house has to be cleaned, inspected and passed."

"Can't I *hire* someone to clean it?"

"No, ma'am, we have our own teams for that."

Donna picked up a pen from the desk in front of her and idly began doodling on a nearby tablet. "*When,* exactly, will it be ready, Lieutenant? Can you tell me that, at least?"

"No, ma'am," he told her.

She was really beginning to hate the word

"ma'am." "How about a hint?" she asked, desperate now.

He chuckled.

Donna snarled silently.

"If I were you, I'd count on Wednesday."

Great. She couldn't move into Jack's apartment at the noncommissioned officers' barracks. Strictly for bachelors. *Her* apartment was in Maryland. Hardly a commuting distance.

She looked around her father's home office and muffled a sigh. Apparently they would be staying with the colonel a few days anyway. Since she and Jack were hardly talking, at least they would have her father as a buffer between them.

Images of the night before, their first night back from Laughlin, swam in front of her eyes. They'd arrived late, with everyone tired from the long drive and even longer silences. Jack had gallantly carried hers and her father's bags into the colonel's house and then promptly disappeared into the night. Oh, he'd mumbled something about going back to the NCO barracks for his things, but Donna recognized an escape attempt when she saw one.

Still, he couldn't get away with staying at the barracks more than one night—not if he expected everyone on base to believe that they were the happily married newlyweds they were pretending to be.

Which brought her back to the problem at hand.

"That's the best you can do?" she asked the beleaguered man on the other end of the phone.

"That's it, ma'am."

Donna cringed. "Thanks very much."

"Yes, ma'am. Oh, and congratulations to you and the first sergeant, ma'am."

Donna hung up and glanced at the notepad. While talking to the lieutenant, her subconscious mind had doodled a gallows, complete with dangling noose and three steps to oblivion.

"Now *there's* a good sign," she muttered. Standing, she tore off the top sheet, crumpled it into a ball and tossed it into the trash can beside the desk.

"Married?" Gunnery Sergeant Tom Haley shook his head, slapped his ear as if he'd heard wrong, and said again, "Married?"

Jack shrugged off his friend's stunned surprise. Tom had been on leave, so hadn't yet heard all of the gossip. Jack figured it would take at least another day for the latest piece of news to sweep across the base. "Will you stop saying that?"

"Sorry," the other man said. "It's just that I never expected to hear you say those words."

"Yeah, well," Jack muttered, "neither did I."

"She must be something." Tom's blond eyebrows lifted high over blue eyes. "Who is she?"

Ah… Finally, the question he'd been dreading. He just knew that the minute his friends found out about him marrying the colonel's daughter, his life would become a living hell.

"Her name's Donna."

"Donna what?"

"Harris." He was stalling and he knew it.

Tom threw a pencil at him from across the room. It missed him, clattering on the linoleum floor. "I know that much. What was it *before* you married her?"

"Why do you care?"

"Is there a reason you don't want me to know her name?"

There was just no way out of this, Jack told himself, and the longer he stalled, the more interested Tom would become. Besides, what was the point? In another day or so, everyone in his world would know. He braced himself for the merciless ragging he was going to take. "Fine. Her name was Candello."

"Candello..." Tom leaned back in his chair, lifted both legs to the corner of his desk and crossed his ankles. Folding his hands atop his chest, he said the name again. "Candello. Now why does—" He stopped. His feet dropped to the floor with a thud and he sat up straight, a wild, disbelieving look in his eyes. "The colonel's daughter?" he finally said. "Are you nuts?"

Certifiable, Jack thought. "Nope," he said out loud. "Just married."

"You gotta be out of your mind, man." Tom jumped up from his chair and walked across the room. With both palms flat on Jack's desk, he leaned in toward his friend. "Don't you know the load of garbage you're gonna have to take because you married a *colonel's* daughter?"

Jack pushed one hand across the top of his head

and leaned back in his chair. Staring up at Tom, he asked, "No, will I really?"

"I didn't even know you knew her," Tom went on.

"Yeah, well, I do."

"Sure, now. But when'd you meet her?"

"Does that—"

"Must have been years ago," Tom said more to himself than to Jack. "Didn't you serve with the colonel back in '90?"

"Yeah…" Of course, he'd never met Donna until a few days ago, but no one else needed to know that.

"Wow." Tom grinned, sat on the edge of Jack's desk and crossed his arms over his chest. "Imagine. *You.* And the colonel's daughter."

Jack frowned to himself. All right, it was unusual. And unexpected. But was it really so damn surprising that Donna Candello might actually find him marriageable?

Then he remembered that he and his blushing bride had agreed not to share a bed, and answered that silent question himself. Okay, the celibacy thing had been his idea. But she had sure agreed quickly enough.

"So?" Tom asked with a broad wink. "Think your daddy-in-law can pull some strings for you? Maybe get you your very own battalion?"

Jack shoved the man off his desk. "Shut up and get to work."

"Wow," Tom said between chuckles, "already, he has delusions of grandeur."

Perfect, he thought as Tom, still laughing, booted up his computer and got back to business. If this was any indication, he was going to have a real good time over the next few days. All because he'd gone outside for a cigarette.

The damn things really would be the death of him.

Donna hadn't been on base in four years.

She sucked in a deep breath, squared her shoulders and dug her fingers into the plush leather of her clutch purse.

Ridiculous to feel so quakey inside. She'd grown up on military bases—at least from the age of thirteen when she'd gone to live with her father. A brief smile crossed her lips and then faded. That had been a tough year, she remembered. Her father and she practically strangers, yet thrust on each other because her mother had suddenly gotten the urge to live in Paris and learn to paint. She'd died only a few years later.

But Donna and her father had gotten past the wary uneasiness. And together they'd found what they had both been missing. Family. Love. Trust.

Donna shuddered. If only she had trusted her father's judgment four years ago, she could have saved herself a truckload of embarrassment—not to mention this marriage that wasn't a marriage.

She lifted her chin and stared at the door not twenty feet from her. Just beyond that doorway, amid a bustle of marines, was her husband's office. Unfortunately, Jack's desk was depressingly close to her father's. Which meant by going inside, she would be forcing herself to face the scene of her grandest error in judgment.

It was right after her engagement had blown up in her face. She'd been feeling fragile and decidedly unwanted—a dangerous combination, as it turned out.

Inside that building was the very desk where she'd tried to seduce her father's assistant, only to have her dad unexpectedly interrupt her sad Mata Hari attempt.

She could still feel the heat of shame rushing into her cheeks. She saw the young corporal's wide, horrified eyes as he'd stared at his commanding officer, and in memory, she would always hear her father's quick intake of breath followed by the disappointed tone of his voice when he'd said her name.

Good Lord. She lifted one hand to shield her eyes as though it might block out the memory. How could she have been so stupid? And as if that wasn't enough, she hadn't even had the guts to stay and brave the situation out. No. Not Donna Candello. She'd jumped the first plane out of town and hadn't shown her face since.

Until now, when she was around just long enough to screw up again.

"Ma'am?" A deep voice came from just to her right.

Donna half turned and looked at the marine staring at her in obvious concern.

"You all right, ma'am?"

"Probably not," she said tiredly. "But thanks for asking."

"Can I help in some way?"

Kind. The lieutenant was just trying to be kind. She knew that. Unfortunately, that didn't change things.

"No, thank you," she said with a small, half-hearted smile. "If there's one thing I don't need at the moment, it's one more marine."

He blinked, surprised, but Donna ignored his confusion and started walking toward the doors. Determined to face her ghosts before she could chicken out again.

Six

Jack glanced up as Tom Haley leapt to his feet, his gaze locked squarely on the doorway. "Can I help you, ma'am?" he said in a tone that was more eager than polite.

"I'm here to see Sergeant Harris," a too familiar female voice answered.

Damn. Instantly it felt as though a lead weight had settled in the pit of Jack's stomach. Yet at the same time a lower portion of his anatomy experienced a far different reaction.

Slowly, he swiveled his head in her direction. "*First* Sergeant," he corrected automatically.

Twin black brows lifted slightly, arching over the dark brown eyes that haunted his sleep. What might have been a smile briefly crossed her lips before she said, "Right."

Damn, why'd she have to look so good? Her deep green blouse, open at the collar, was tucked into the narrow waistband of a short black skirt that skimmed her hips like a lover's hands only to flare out and swing about her thighs as she walked farther into the room. The tap of her high heels against the linoleum sounded like a heartbeat. Those legs of hers could be registered as weapons. As for her eyes...well, Jack didn't even want to *think* about them for the moment.

Tom cleared his throat dramatically, bringing Jack back from fantasies he shouldn't be indulging in anyway. Shooting his friend a frosty look, he scowled when Tom only grinned at him.

Apparently the man had no intention of going anywhere without an introduction. Standing, Jack said stiffly, "Donna, this is Gunnery Sergeant Haley—"

"Tom," the other man interrupted with a smile that looked entirely too friendly.

Frowning, Jack finished the introduction. "Tom, this is my *wife*. Donna."

All right, saying that word felt strange, but at the same time, he really didn't like the look in Tom Haley's eyes as the man studied Donna from head to toe. Though why all of a sudden Tom's charm with women should bother him, he didn't want to consider.

"It's a pleasure, Mrs. Harris," Tom said as he came out from behind his desk and crossed the room to her, one hand extended in welcome.

Donna placed her hand in his and said, "Please. Call me Donna."

Jack frowned to himself as his gaze landed on their joined hands. He couldn't help noticing that Tom held hers for just a bit longer than necessary.

His stomach churned and he knew it wasn't because of the rot-gut coffee he'd been pouring down his throat all morning. Damn it, wasn't it enough that he had to deal with Donna privately? Did she *have* to show up at his office, too?

But even as that thought crossed his mind, he had to admit that it wasn't just her presence that upset his peace of mind. It was her. Period. Ever since that first morning when she'd faced him down despite an obviously painful hangover, he'd been intrigued. Okay, he admitted silently, *more* than intrigued.

Sober, she was even more disturbing.

Gritting his teeth, he forced himself to ask calmly. "Is there a problem?"

Donna flicked him a quick look. One eyebrow lifted slightly. "Just because a wife comes to her *husband's* office, does there have to be a problem?"

"Yeah, Jack." Tom joined in, guiding her to a chair. "Lighten up. Maybe she just missed you."

"Yeah," Donna agreed. "Maybe that's why I'm here. I missed you."

Sure. Like she'd missed a toothache. But he couldn't very well say that in front of Tom. Not if they were going to keep up the pretense of being happy newlyweds.

She sat and crossed one incredible leg over the

other. Her black stockings brushed against each other and the hem of her skirt fell back, displaying far more leg than Jack wanted Tom to see.

Turning to his friend, he snapped, "Don't you have somewhere you have to be?"

"Nope," Tom assured him, perching one hip on the edge of his desk.

Donna smiled at the man before turning her dark eyes back to Jack. He wasn't blind to the fact that her smile disappeared at the same instant.

"Look, Donna," he said, trying to keep his voice even and his gaze away from her upper thigh. "If it's not important, I've got work to take care of."

"Of course it's important," she said. Swinging her right foot gently, effectively drawing his gaze back to her legs, she went on. "I've been talking to base housing and—"

"You shouldn't have to do that," Tom cut in, reaching out to briefly stroke one of Donna's hands. "Jack, why don't you take care of all that for her?"

"Because," he said tightly, "I've got other things to do." Silently he wondered how many bones in Tom's hand he could break with one quick move. Thankfully, the other man retreated, so it wasn't put to the test.

Donna stiffened slightly. "And I don't, you mean?"

"I didn't say that," he countered, meeting her dark eyes evenly. "It's just that I have a job to do and—"

"And I'm unemployed?" she finished for him.

Hell, he didn't even *know* if she had a job or not.

"It wasn't an accusation," he said.

"I happen to have a very good job," she told him, squaring her shoulders and lifting her chin just a bit higher.

"Really?" Tom interjected, pulling those eyes of hers to him. "Where do you work?"

She paused for a long minute, bit her lip, then answered, "Maryland."

"Kind of a long commute," Jack said.

Her gaze flicked to him instantly. Then, as if remembering Tom's presence, she plastered a smile on her face and cooed, "Naturally, I'll have to resign. I hadn't expected to spend my vacation being swept away by passion."

Passion. The only thing she'd been swept away by was a pitcher of margaritas...which they were both paying for.

"I'm sure you'll find another job soon," Tom assured her soothingly, managing to irritate Jack at the same time.

A long silence filled the passing moments until finally, Tom pushed up from the desk, smiled at Donna and completely ignored his longtime friend. "I still say, if I had a wife as pretty as yours, Jack, I'd be doing everything I could to help her get settled in on base."

And the chances of Tom Haley *ever* settling down with one woman were slimmer than Jack's chances of being an astronaut.

"Thank you, Tom," Donna said, giving him a

wide, bright smile. One, Jack thought, she hadn't seen fit to bestow on the man who'd saved her reputation and her father's.

"You need anything, you just give me a call," Tom told her before gathering up a stack of papers from the edge of his desk. "And now, if you'll excuse me, maybe there *are* a few things I should be doing."

Once he was gone, Jack turned to her. "What the hell was that all about?"

"What?" She shrugged, her foot swinging at a bit faster pace. "Your friend was just being nice. So was I."

"Any nicer and he would have—" He interrupted himself, not wanting to go down that particular road.

"Jealous?" she asked.

That stung. "Now, why would I be jealous?"

"That's what I was wondering."

"Well, don't," he said quickly. "All I meant was, if we're supposed to be happily married, you shouldn't flirt with the biggest ladies' man on base."

"I wasn't flirting," she snapped.

"What do you call crossing your legs and swinging your foot like that?"

She shook her head. "I call it crossing my legs and swinging my foot."

He rubbed one hand over his face and fought for control. Ridiculous. He knew he was overreacting and still he couldn't seem to stop himself. But, damn it, watching Tom Haley watching Donna had been…unsettling.

Why that was, he didn't want to explore.

"Fine," he finally said. "Let's just forget it, shall we?"

She gave him a slow, thoughtful nod.

"What are you doing here, anyway?"

"We have to talk about our living arrangements."

"Now?"

"Yes, now." She stood and crossed the room to him. "I've been on the phone with Base Housing most of the morning. They say there's a house available but we can't have it for another two or three days."

Perfect. Just three days until he and Donna were actually living together. Well, he'd better find a way to control his hormones before then. "Fine. What's the problem?"

"The problem is, you can't stay at your apartment in the NCO barracks until then."

No, he couldn't. He'd known the night before that it would be his last night in the place. And frankly, he wasn't going to miss it much. A small place, it wasn't exactly anyone's idea of home sweet home.

"Unless of course," she said hesitantly. "I can stay there with you."

"No. Bachelors only."

She shrugged and nodded as if she'd been expecting that answer. "So we're left with two options."

"Yeah?" He had a feeling he wasn't going to like either of them.

"We can go off base and stay in a motel, or we can stay with my father at his house."

Faced with those two choices, he made the obvious call. "I vote motel."

She smiled briefly. "Somehow, I thought you would. But then people would wonder why we weren't staying with Dad."

"So," he said, "let them wonder."

Cocking her head to one side, she looked up at him. "This marriage was *your* idea, Jack. To keep people from wondering. Talking. Remember?"

Yeah, he remembered. All too clearly. It had seemed like such a good idea at the time.

"Fine." He knew when he was beaten. "The colonel's house, it is."

"Relax, Jack," Donna told him. "Your virtue's safe with me. It's a four-bedroom house. We don't *have* to share a room."

He glanced at her and Donna tried to read the emotions glimmering in his gray eyes. But she couldn't. Either he was a master at masking his feelings, or she just didn't know him well enough yet. And what did *that* say about the situation? She didn't know him well enough to tell what he was thinking, but she *did* know him well enough to marry?

Good God.

"That was the deal," he reminded her. "A platonic marriage. Easier on both of us."

Well, on one of us, anyway, she thought, letting her gaze skim down her new husband's trim, muscular body. Speaking as a twenty-eight-year-old married virgin, sharing a bed might not be so bad.

Heat suddenly rushed to her cheeks. She could hardly believe what she was thinking. A few days ago she hadn't known this man from Adam. Now not only was she married to him, she was entertaining fantasies of midnight romps in the hay.

Sucking in a deep breath, she nodded. "Yeah. Easier."

"So is that all you wanted?" he asked.

Now there was a loaded question. But she ignored the opening and simply answered, "Yes. That's all."

"Okay, then," Jack said, rubbing the back of his neck, "I guess I'll—"

"Sure." She cut him off neatly. "I'll let you get back to work. Since you are the only one with a job."

"Look," he said. "I'm sorry about that. I didn't know about your job."

"What? You thought I was independently wealthy?" She shook her head. "Sorry to disappoint you, but you didn't marry an heiress."

"That's not what I meant."

"What did you mean, Jack?"

"Hell if I know."

She inhaled slowly, deeply, needing a minute or two to steady herself. For heaven's sake, why was she baiting the man? It wasn't *his* fault that they were in this mess. The only reason they were married at all was that she was too much of a coward to face her father after the mess she'd created four years before.

Now, instead of trying to make the best of an impossible situation, she was doing her utmost to be as difficult as possible. Real smart.

"Donna—"

"Jack—"

They spoke at the same time, then looked at each other for a long moment in sheepish silence.

"You want me to walk you out?" he finally asked.

"No, thanks. I know the way."

"Are you going to stop in and see your father?"

No way, she thought. She was not ready to walk past the desk where she'd once made a complete ass of herself.

She shook her head and dug her fingers into her purse. But neither did she want to explain her reasons to a husband who wouldn't be around for more than a few months. The fewer people who knew of that little episode, the better.

"I'll see him tonight," she said. "He's probably busy, anyway." Then she turned and headed for the door. With every step she took, Donna felt his gaze burning into her back. Heat snaked through her bloodstream, warming her from the inside out. Her knees trembled. Her high heels suddenly felt precarious. Just before she left the room, his voice stopped her.

"Donna?"

"Yes?" She half turned to face him, hoping he couldn't see the flush of heat no doubt staining her cheeks. That inscrutable look was on his face again and she wished heartily that she could read minds.

"This will all work out. All we have to do is settle in. We'll get used to each other."

Sure, she thought. All she had to do was train her heartbeat not to jump into double time when she saw him. And, if she could just keep reminding herself that sex hadn't been part of their deal, that would be a big help, too. In this case, she wasn't sure if being a virgin was a help or a hindrance. Never having been intimate with a man, she couldn't miss what she'd never had. On the other hand, her fantasies weren't based on reality, so her mind had free rein in coming up with wild imaginings designed to torture the lovelorn.

Lord, she was in trouble.

Donna gave him what she hoped was a carefree smile and lifted one hand in a brief wave. "Of course we'll get used to each other, Jack. It's just a matter of time."

He would never get used to this, Jack told himself as he lay wide awake in one of the colonel's guest bedrooms. Dinner had been a disaster, even though his superior officer had done everything to make him more comfortable. The colonel had made an issue of taking off his uniform blouse and telling Jack to do the same. Then, with both of them in plain white T-shirts, Colonel Candello had assured him that inside that house, there were no ranks.

Though Jack appreciated the gesture, he still

hadn't been able to get comfortable. Not with Donna sitting directly across the table from him. Damn it, even in an old T-shirt and cutoffs, she looked good enough to stop his heart.

Grumbling to himself, he sat up, punched his pillow into shape and lay down again. Wide awake, he turned his head toward the window where a silver strand of moonlight poured through the half-open drapes.

His brain wandered aimlessly, conjuring up image after image of Donna. What the hell had he gotten himself into? And how was he ever going to survive a platonic marriage that was already making him nuts?

From the next room he heard the soft, unmistakable sound of Donna humming in her sleep. Apparently she wasn't having any problem at all adjusting to this frustrating situation.

Groaning, he yanked the pillow out from under his head, slammed it down over his face and prayed for sleep that wouldn't come.

"It's so small," Donna said, and heard the whine in her voice. But the house was so dismal, she couldn't help herself.

"It's big enough for us," Jack told her, strolling across the eight-foot-wide living room into the tiny kitchen.

Donna followed him, hesitantly poking her head around the corner to inspect a kitchen almost too small for the appliances it held. "You're kidding," she muttered, her gaze landing on a refrigerator that looked to be an antique. "Does it require a block of ice to keep things cool?" she wondered out loud, only half kidding.

He slapped one palm against the short, scarred fridge. "It's not *that* old."

"It's beyond old. Closing in on 'archeological relic.'"

Jack slapped it again, as if to prove her wrong, and the machine groaned, gurgled and shook on its four metal feet.

"I think you killed it," Donna whispered, half expecting the blasted thing to explode.

"It's a marine refrigerator," Jack told her, taking one step back from the still-shaking appliance. "It's not dead. It's regrouping."

"Ooo-rah," she muttered, and let her gaze slide away from the quivering fridge to the two long cupboards, a stove that told her she'd be doing a lot of barbecuing, and a sink that had more gouges and scars ripped into its porcelain surface than most tanks saw in a lifetime. Wonderful, she thought, and glanced at the faded, drooping curtains over the one tiny window. The blue-and-white-checked gingham hung limply, its starch long gone, along with most of its color.

As she watched, Jack reached up and pushed the curtains back, allowing a narrow shaft of sunlight to slide through the glass. An instant later the curtain rod dropped from its hardware and clattered into the sink.

Donna jumped.

Jack's eyebrows lifted.

Stepping up behind him, she glanced down at the fallen curtains spilling over the rim of the sink, then up at Jack. "Nice," she said. "And to think, it passed inspection."

He frowned slightly, picked up the short rod and inspected it. "Not a problem. I can fix this."

A full-time handyman wouldn't be able to fix this place, she thought. Not without twenty years at his disposal.

"So, *First* Sergeant," Donna said thoughtfully, "this is the house your rank has earned you."

He slanted a look at her. "Actually, no. But this is all that was available, remember?"

True, Donna thought, her gaze sliding from his to roam over her temporary home. She suppressed a shudder. Every wall in the place was painted the same shade of eggshell white. Apparently, the corps painters lacked imagination. She reached out to touch one of the kitchen walls and wondered idly just how many layers of latex paint actually covered it.

And how many families had lived there? How many kids had scrawled their names on these walls in crayon only to have them painted over? A wistful smile crossed her face briefly as she recalled the years she'd spent growing up on military bases. It hadn't been easy, she thought, but at the same time, there had always been a sense of community.

Glancing at Jack, she fought a twinge of regret that their marriage was nothing more than pretense. She'd wanted a family of her own for so long. And now that she finally had a husband, it was only temporary.

"I know it's not much," he was saying, "but we won't need the place for long, anyway."

She nodded and walked off, headed for the incredibly short hallway that led to two bedrooms and the bathroom. Jack's footsteps sounded right behind her. But she hadn't had to hear him to know he was near. She felt his presence in every cell of her body. Which was probably not a good thing.

"Look, Donna," he said softly, and she half turned to face him. "I know this isn't quite up to what you're used to, but—"

"I know," she interrupted, "it's only temporary." Shifting her gaze again, she inspected the place slowly. "But je-ezz, Jack, how can the marine corps expect people to live in shacks like this?"

He stiffened a bit at the slur on the corps, but to give him his due, he shrugged and nodded. "They don't, really." Lifting his gaze to the patched, water-stained ceiling, he went on. "All of these old places are scheduled for demolition in the next couple of years."

An unexpected splinter of regret shot through her. Lord knew the house was in sad shape. Still, the little place had sheltered hundreds of families. Didn't that count for something, too? Silly, but she felt the sting of tears tickle the backs of her eyes. To cover up her sudden twist of emotion, she said, "If they don't fall down first."

Jack's features tightened briefly before relaxing. "Yeah, I guess. So, which room do you want?"

It didn't matter, so Donna waved one hand to the room on the right. "This one will be fine."

"Okay, then," Jack said. "I'll bring in my stuff, then we'll go to your father's house and pick up the rest."

Until her things arrived from Maryland, Donna's father was loaning them an extra bed and a few of his furnishings.

Leaning up against the wall, Donna asked, "So what do you think the neighbors will say when they watch us carry in two beds?"

He rubbed the back of his neck, a habit Donna had already noticed.

"Probably nothing. They'll just assume one of the rooms is for a guest room."

He was right, she thought. After all, who would ever guess that happily married newlyweds weren't even sharing a bedroom?

Seven

Donna stood on the front porch of the colonel's residence and watched Jack load furniture into the back of a borrowed pickup. Two of her father's lamps, a box spring and mattress, a dresser, and one small coffee table filled the compact truck bed.

She inhaled sharply, blew all of the air out, and deliberately fixed her gaze on her husband. The pale blue T-shirt he'd tucked into faded blue jeans stretched and pulled across his muscular chest and shoulders. He placed a hand on the edge of the truck bed and in one fluid motion, jumped inside to secure their cargo.

Shaking her head, she told herself not to notice the curve of his behind as he bent to straighten something. He'd made it clear from the beginning that he wasn't interested in pursuing anything other than a platonic relationship with her. The least she could do was stop drooling over him and save herself from any further embarrassment.

"You okay?" her father asked as he stepped up behind her on the porch.

"Sure," she said, forcing a brightness she didn't feel into her voice. "Why wouldn't I be?"

"The First Sergeant's a good man, Donna."

She half turned to look up at him, saw the gentleness in his eyes and looked away again, before she could cry. "I really screwed up big time, didn't I?"

Easing one hip against the porch railing, he lifted a hand to smooth the hair back from her face. Donna risked a quick glance at him and saw the same love and understanding she'd always found in his eyes.

As she watched him, he smiled briefly. "Let's just say, this was one of your more memorable achievements."

Donna groaned quietly. "And to think all of this started because I was too embarrassed to face you."

"Now, that," he said. "I don't understand. Why would you feel like that, Donna?"

Why? Because she could still see the look on his face when he had walked in on the most embarrassing moment of her life.

"I've missed seeing you," he said softly.

Her heart twisted and the backs of her eyes stung as she walked into her father's arms. She felt the warm, solid strength of him as he held her just as he had so many times during her adolescence. "Oh,

Daddy, I've missed you, too. Three or four phone calls a week just isn't enough, I guess."

"Then why didn't you ever come home?" He pulled back and looked down at her. "God knows, I begged for a visit often enough."

"I just couldn't bring myself to face you." She sniffed and took a step back. "News flash. Big Strong Marine Has Coward For Daughter."

"You're not a coward, Donna."

"What would you call it?"

"Impetuous?" he suggested with a grin.

She wiped her eyes and gave him a small smile.

"Don't you know I love you?"

"Of course I do," she said, though silently she admitted that it was good to hear him confirm it. "But even Job had limits. Didn't he?"

Tom Candello chuckled and shook his head. "No father has limits. Not where his little girl's concerned."

She took a deep breath and looked at him. Donna had missed seeing him. Visiting him. But in four years she'd never been able to work up the nerve to look him in the eye. "Not even when he walks into his office to find his daughter trying desperately to seduce a corporal, who in turn was trying desperately to escape?"

His smile faded, but the light in his eyes didn't dim a fraction. "Not even then."

Relief poured through her. She'd been so ashamed. So humiliated. *Why* hadn't she gone to him that night at the ball instead of looking for courage at the bottom of a margarita pitcher? If only she'd used her brain, she wouldn't have traded one mess for another, bigger one.

"God," she muttered, disgusted with herself. "I'm an idiot."

Her father laughed gently. "You *do* have some interesting moments."

"Interesting. That's one word for them."

"Don't be so hard on yourself, honey."

"Why not?" she asked. "Not only did I screw things up for myself this time, but I dragged Jack along with me."

The colonel turned his head to look at the other man. "Jack's a big boy. He knew what he was doing."

"Did he, Daddy?" Donna waited until her father's gaze had shifted back to her. "The man *married* me, for God's sake."

"It was his idea."

"Yeah," she agreed. "One I'm sure he's regretted every moment since."

Her father frowned slightly. "Has he said so?"

"No," she said quickly, not wanting her father to think Jack was being anything less than damned nice about this whole thing. "Actually, he seems fine with the situation." Except of course, she added silently, for the fact that he wants nothing physical to do with his temporary wife.

"Then why don't you relax?" her father asked.

"How am I supposed to do that?" she demanded.

"Just try not to make everything so hard. It doesn't have to be."

"Easy for you to say," she muttered, glancing back at her husband's tush as he backed his way out of the truck.

The colonel reached up, grabbed a lock of her hair and gave it a gentle tug. She looked at him.

"Donna, give yourself—and Jack—a chance. Who knows? You two might end up *enjoying* being married."

"Sure and what color blue do you think the sun will be tomorrow?"

He shook his head and stood beside her. "All I'm saying is, as long as you're married—make the best of the situation. You didn't trap Jack into a marriage. He volunteered for this mission."

"Yeah," she said on a sigh. "And him without a bazooka."

"Cut it out," her father snapped, and her gaze shot to his. "Make the best of this, Donna. Don't throw away what might turn out to be a blessing because you're too proud, or stubborn, or whatever, to admit that you actually *like* Jack Harris."

"Don't you get it, Dad?" she countered quickly. "It doesn't matter if I like him or not. He's not interested. Hell, I'm not even sure *I* am."

"He's not Kyle."

"No, he's not," Donna said, tossing another glance at the man she'd married only days before. "Jack didn't sleep with my maid of honor two days before the wedding. Heck, he doesn't even want to sleep with—'' She broke off quickly. Heat rushed to her cheeks as she realized that she was talking to her *father* about her lack of a sex life. Lord, when would she learn to shut up?

Thankfully, her father let that statement go, apparently just as eager to avoid such a talk as she was.

"Donna," he said, taking her by the shoulders and turning her to face him. "Sometimes, life's little surprises turn out to be the best thing that you could hope for."

"And sometimes, it's just another screwup by Donna Candello."

"Donna Harris."

She groaned.

Her father shook his head and pulled her close for a brief, hard hug. When she stepped back, she looked up at him hopefully. "I don't suppose you'd be interested in coming over for dinner tonight? Kind of help ease us into this moving-in-together thing?"

"Sorry," he said. "I can't. I think I may have a date."

Her eyebrows lifted. Her father had hardly *ever* dated. "You 'think' you 'may' have a date?"

He nodded as his gaze moved past her to stare out into the side yard. "It's a little iffy right now."

"Who is she?"

He shook his head, meeting her eyes briefly. "I'll tell you that if I can actually convince her to go out with me."

"Why wouldn't she?" Donna demanded. "You're smart, handsome, funny, kind—''

"Thanks for the vote of confidence," her father interrupted, laughing. "But why don't you let me handle my love life and you concentrate on your own?"

"Yours would be easier."

"What was that you said about cowardice?"

"Guilty."

The colonel turned his head slightly. "Looks like Jack's ready to go."

Donna looked up to see her husband moving toward them, and told herself once again not to notice how well those jeans fit his long legs. Oh, she was in deep water here, and there was no one around to throw her a life preserver.

She started reluctantly for the steps, then stopped suddenly as if something had occurred to her. "Dad?"

"Yes?"

"What ever happened to the corporal?"

Thankfully, he knew instantly who she was referring to. "You scared the poor kid to death. He requested a transfer almost immediately."

Donna grimaced. "To where?"

"Greenland. I think he wanted to get as far away from here as possible."

"You mean," she clarified unnecessarily, "from me."

"Donna…"

"Some seductress," she muttered more to herself than her father. "Come on to a man and he runs thousands of miles in the opposite direction."

As she walked down the sidewalk, she met Jack's gaze and felt another flutter of awareness streak through her. He waved to the colonel, then took her arm to escort her to the truck. And Donna couldn't help but wonder if her husband would scare off as easily as that corporal had.

More important, did she have the nerve to find out?

Jack dismissed the private he'd enlisted to help move furniture, then stood back and surveyed his new bedroom. Donna was right. The place was small. And old. And falling apart. But it had one definite plus. It wasn't in the NCO barracks.

"Jack," Donna called from the other room.

On the down side, he was living with a wife he wasn't allowed to touch. "Yeah?"

"Can you come here for a minute?"

Steeling himself against the sight of Donna's bare legs and nicely rounded butt, Jack headed for her bedroom. Evidently it didn't matter how prepared he was. One look at her and his body tightened like an overtuned guitar string.

He stood in the doorway, watching her as she struggled and yanked at one of two windows. Half bent over in her effort to shove the window open, her cutoffs crept high on her thighs, the worn fabric stretching dangerously thin across her curves. The midriff-length T-shirt she wore rode up on her back, displaying even more of her deliciously smooth, ivory skin.

His teeth ground together as he struggled to hold on to what little self-control he had left. "What do you need?" he asked.

She shot him a harried look over her shoulder and blew a lock of dark hair out of her eyes. "Help."

He chuckled despite the pain in his lower body.

"This isn't funny," she told him, narrowing the one eye she had locked on him. "Somebody must have nailed this darn thing shut." She grunted for good measure as she gave the window another shove. Nothing.

Sighing heavily, she straightened and glared at the closed window, while idly rubbing a spot on her lower back.

Before he could do something stupid like offer to massage her strained muscles, he walked around the edge of her bed and straight to the window. Slowly, he inspected the wooden frame, giving himself time to adjust to the nearness of her. Damn. What kind of woman wore perfume to move furniture?

Obviously, he told himself as he breathed in the soft, floral scent, *this* one.

Keep centered, he warned himself. Mind on the job.

"It's not nailed shut," he said over his shoulder. "It's just been painted over."

"Perfect."

"If you'll get me a knife, I'll open it for you."

"Deal."

Brushing up against him, she mumbled, "Sorry," as she squeezed past and headed for the kitchen.

That incredibly brief touch shouldn't have been enough to start a wildfire in his blood. But it had. Setting both hands flat on either side of the window, Jack let his head fall forward until his chin hit his neck. Closing his eyes, he concentrated the iron will he was known for to defeat this completely irrational hormonal attraction for his wife.

Hell, he didn't even like her much. Well, all right, he liked her more than he had thought he would. But she still managed to give the impression that she was visiting royalty and he was a lucky, though unworthy, peasant to be allowed in her presence.

Just her attitude about this house was enough to underline all of the differences between them. He could tell by looking at her that she was disgusted to have to live in the place.

He lifted his head and looked out the window to the backyard. Knee-high, burned brown grass covered the lot, but there was a single, scrawny tree in the far corner and plenty of possibilities. He was willing to admit that the little house wasn't much, but it was the first *home* he'd lived in since his parents had died when he was a kid.

The aunt and uncle he'd stayed with after the car accident had lived in an apartment and hadn't exactly been the Ward and June Cleaver types. They hadn't abused him or anything, though. In fact, they'd hardly noticed him at all until he'd turned sixteen and landed a part-time job. And even then, they'd only really been interested in his pathetically small paycheck.

Gritting his teeth, he pushed all of those memories to the deepest, darkest corner of his mind. That was over. That life was so far behind him, even the memories usually couldn't catch him. But he'd been doing too much thinking lately. And that was her fault.

"Sorry it took me so long," she said as she came back into the room.

Jack dismissed the past and focused on his present. "No problem."

"I couldn't find a sharp knife," she went on as if he hadn't spoken, and didn't stop walking until she was right beside him. "Will this one be all right?"

A butter knife with a bent blade wasn't exactly a precision tool, but he'd make do. He wanted to pry up the window and get the hell out of her bedroom as quickly as possible. "Yeah, it's fine."

His fingers closed over the knife handle, brushing against hers as she handed it to him. He swore he actually *saw* bright blue sparks rise from where they touched. He damn sure *felt* the sizzle. Right down to the soles of his feet.

Before he could blatantly ignore it, though, Donna took one long step back from him and put her hands behind her back for good measure.

His grip on the knife tightened as he deliberately turned to the task at hand. Running the blade along the painted-over seam, he cracked away the latest layer of white paint until the sash was free. Then he gave a hard shove and pushed the window open.

Instantly, a cold wind rushed in, carrying the scent

of the sea. Donna inhaled sharply and smiled. "Isn't that great?"

"Yeah. But cold."

She grinned up at him. "Cold, yes. But not freezing. I talked to my old roommate this morning and she told me Baltimore got hit by a blizzard last night."

The weather, he thought. They were actually discussing the weather.

Trying for a different subject, he asked, "So, was your roommate mad about you getting married and skipping out on your share of the rent?"

She shook her head. "Mad? No. Surprised? Yes. But it's working out all right. She had wanted her boyfriend to move in anyway."

"Handy," he said for lack of anything better.

"Yeah," Donna agreed with a ridiculously over-bright smile. "All's well that ends well."

A long moment of silence stretched out between them.

She shivered slightly in the blast of cold air coming in the window. Jack lowered it several inches.

"Uh, do you want me to do the other window, too?"

Her smile faded as she shook her head. "No, one window's enough for today. I would like it if you could find the switch on that refrigerator and turn it on. Though I'm still not sure it actually works with electricity."

"No problem," he told her, already moving, grateful for a reason to escape the too close confines of her bedroom.

"You always say that, you know."

"Say what?"

"No problem. Isn't anything a problem for you, Jack?"

He only had one at the moment. Keeping his hands off his wife. But all he said was, "Any problem can be handled." He hoped.

"Before you go—" Her voice stopped him just inches from a clean getaway. He turned in the doorway and waited. "What is that?" she asked, pointing to the ceiling.

His gaze followed hers, then narrowed on an odd-shaped plaster bubble. Why hadn't he noticed that earlier? he wondered, then knew the answer. He'd been keeping his gaze down, trying to avoid staring at Donna. He took a step closer, tilted his head to one side and studied the plaster oddity for a long minute before admitting, "I don't know."

"It's right over my bed," she observed unnecessarily.

He tossed her a glance. "You want to switch rooms?"

She looked around at the few things she'd already unpacked and he could tell she didn't want to move any of it again. To reassure her, he took another look at the warped ceiling. "It's probably just that the plaster's gotten damp over the years. Most likely, the repair crews just keep slapping more plaster on it every year until it looks like a blister."

"A blister," she mused thoughtfully. "Yeah. That's exactly what it looks like. Or maybe a pimple."

"So, you're okay with this?"

She glanced at him and nodded. "Sure. I mean, if it's been this way for years, what are the chances it's going to pop on me?"

He jerked her a brief nod, then said, "I'll go get the fridge going."

He only hoped the old appliance would be as adept at running as he was quickly becoming.

After sharing a frozen pizza and a cheap bottle of wine they'd picked up at the commissary, Donna and Jack retreated to their own bedrooms.

Lying wide awake in the moon-washed darkness, Donna stared blankly up at the plaster pimple on her ceiling. Her father's words kept repeating over and over again in her mind.

It was tempting, she thought. The idea of treating this pretend marriage like a real one. After all, she was twenty-eight years old. If she was ever going to have a husband and kids, she'd have to start sometime soon. And Jack seemed like a nice guy. Hadn't he leaped into the fray to rescue her father's reputation? Wasn't he being a good sport about living in this miserable little hut?

And...didn't she get goose pimples just watching him walk across a room?

Sighing, Donna resettled more deeply into her pillow. None of this mattered, she told herself. Because

Jack had already made it painfully clear that he wasn't interested in anything more than a temporary marriage. So it was pointless for her to daydream about other, more pleasant possibilities.

Wasn't it?

These thoughts were getting her nowhere. And now she had the extra added bonus of a deep, unsettling ache building slowly inside her.

Her gaze locked on the stupid pimple hanging over her bed. How hard would it have been for the contractors employed by the corps to just *fix* the ceiling?

Scowling and muttering darkly to herself, Donna stood on the mattress, directly under the giant pimple. Tilting her head back, she examined the darn thing as closely as she could. Finally she reached up and gingerly poked at the white, crinkly plaster.

Instantly the ceiling exploded.

What must have been oceans of water and tons of wet plaster dropped on her.

She screamed and ducked.

Jack bolted out of bed as if he'd been shot. Donna! He took the pitifully few steps that separated their bedrooms and threw her door open. Stunned at the disaster in front of him, he raced barefoot across the chunks of wet plaster and absently noted the sound of the rug squishing beneath his feet.

Bracing one knee on the waterlogged bed, he grabbed Donna and yanked her off the mattress. Holding her tightly, he demanded, "Are you all right?"

Slowly she lifted her head, then reached up and pushed her soaking wet hair off her forehead. Plucking a piece of plaster off her lips, she nodded. ''I think so.''

''What happened?'' he asked, even though he could see for himself that the damn ceiling had come down on top of her. He never should have let her take that room. He should have insisted on sleeping in there himself. She could have been killed.

''I popped the pimple,'' Donna said, half turning in his arms to survey the damage.

''You popped it?''

''I swear. All I did was touch it. And *boom!* Just touched it. That's all,'' she said, her voice sounding faint, as if coming from a distance.

His heart racing, Jack pulled her closely to him. His arms closed around her and he ran his hands up and down her body, telling himself he was simply checking her for injuries. But she seemed all too healthy.

''Honestly,'' she was saying. ''I don't know what happened. One minute everything was fine and the next minute, the world blew up.''

''It's okay,'' he told her. ''I'll call base housing in the morning. See about getting it repaired.''

She pulled back in his arms and looked up at him. Bits of plaster clung to her wet hair like an abstract crown, and her face was pale. ''Guess our two-bedroom apartment just became a one-bedroom, huh?''

Jack stared at her, admiration rising in his chest.

She was amazing. Her ceiling blows up in her face and there's no hysterics. No crying. Damn it, he didn't want to like her. He really didn't. He could deal with wanting her and not having her. But blast everything, if he liked her, too, it would be too much.

His gaze slipped over her quickly. And just as quickly, he wished he hadn't looked. Her nightgown, God help him, was soaked through, outlining and defining every one of her curves. His body reacted immediately and he took a half step back. Standing there wearing nothing more than his military-issue boxers and his dog tags, he suddenly felt every bit as exposed as she must.

Running one hand over the back of his neck, he shifted his gaze to the wreckage that was her room. "We'll deal with this tomorrow. For tonight, you'll sleep with me."

He glanced at her in time to see one dark eyebrow lift into a high arch.

"I'm not suggesting anything more than sleep," he said, determined that she not think he was using this situation to his own benefit. "We're adults. We can share a bed without sharing anything else."

"I suppose so," she said quietly, picking her sodden nightgown off her chest with her fingertips. Stepping past him into the hall, she added, so quietly he almost missed it, "Seems like a waste of a good bed, though."

Eight

It was more than a waste, Jack thought much later. It was damned torture.

Donna hummed tunelessly as she slipped into a deeper sleep. He turned his head on the pillow to glare at her. How in the hell could she sleep when only inches of mattress separated them?

But as that thought shot through his brain, he realized the answer. She wasn't bothered by his nearness because she simply didn't want him the way he wanted her. Hot. Sweaty. Moaning.

He threw one arm across his eyes and tried to wipe that particular image out of his brain. Hell, he'd never get to sleep otherwise. Scooting over a bit more, he clung to the edge of the mattress, trying to keep as much space between them as possible without actually falling off the bed.

If he had known that this temporary marriage was going to be so blasted hard, he never would have offered to go through with it. He snorted a muffled laugh. Who was he trying to kid? He would have married her, anyway. So what kind of a nut did that make him?

A nut destined for long, frustrating nights. Because he could admit, if only to himself, that from the moment he'd laid eyes on Donna Candello trying to sneak into the ball, he'd wanted her as he'd never wanted anything else in his life.

Two days later Jack was still telling himself that he must have heard her wrong. No way would Donna Candello be interested in him. Okay, fine, she had married him. But that was different. That had been desperation talking. And guilt screaming.

He glanced across the room to where Donna sat curled up on one end of the couch, thumbing through a magazine. She licked her forefinger before turning the page and Jack's insides tightened. His gaze locked on her mouth. He found himself hoping she'd do it again. Breath held, he waited while she perused the page, then slowly lifted her right hand to her lips.

Her tongue darted out and smoothed across her fingertip in an unconsciously seductive manner.

Jack swallowed heavily, closed his eyes and tried to ignore a throbbing ache low in his body with which he was becoming all too familiar.

What if she *had* said what he'd thought she'd said—about wasting a perfectly good bed? She couldn't have meant anything about him specifically. He was not the kind of man she would be interested in. They had absolutely nothing in common. So why did he want her so badly? And where did that leave him? Was he supposed to be the one to go back on their agreement? Hell, it had been his idea to make this a platonic marriage. He couldn't just up and announce that he'd changed his mind, could he?

"Change your mind, Jack?" Donna asked.

"Huh?" He blinked, startled at her mind reading abilities. Just to be sure, though, he asked, "About what?"

She waved one hand at the file folder on the coffee table in front of him. "I thought you said you were going to get those reports done tonight."

That had been the plan. Unfortunately, he couldn't keep his mind on any figures other than hers.

"Nah. Do 'em in the morning."

She frowned at him. "Are you all right?"

Dandy, he thought. "Yeah. Fine."

She didn't look convinced. "Something is wrong," she said. "Still getting ribbed about marrying the colonel's daughter?"

"Not too much," he told her, and didn't add that he was never ribbed by the same man twice. Once some joker faced Jack's steely gray stare, he seemed reluctant to try it again. In general, the hoo-hah was dying down, just as he had predicted it would.

Of course, if he and Donna hadn't gotten married so quickly, the gossip would never have eased off.

And, if they hadn't gotten married, he might be a well-rested man right now. Certainly, he wouldn't be questioning his own sanity.

"You know," she said quietly, "you never did tell me what debt you owed my father that required such a huge payback as marrying me."

Now it was his turn to frown. "Yeah, I know."

Donna studied him for a long minute. This husband of hers was a study in contrasts. Tough, rule-following marine by day. Touchy, skittish husband by night. They'd managed to live together for nearly a week now without killing each other and she was quite sure she was the only one suffering from bouts of near fatal attraction. Little by little, she was coming to know him and yet she knew that there was a big part of himself that he kept hidden...tucked away.

She wanted to reach that part of him and didn't even bother to ask herself why it was so important to her.

"So?" she prompted. "Aren't you going to tell me?"

"Hadn't planned on it," he admitted, standing and walking to the window that overlooked the street. Planting both hands on the wall at either side of the window, he stared quietly out at the darkness.

"Jack," she said, half turning to look at his broad back and rigid stance.

"You want to know why?" he muttered thickly,

his voice rough and harsh as it grated over clearly unpleasant memories. "All right, I'll tell you."

Donna almost stopped him. Almost. She didn't like the way he was holding his shoulders. Stiff, yet hunched, as if expecting a blow. But her instinct was to draw him out. To find out more about the man she had married in such a hurry.

"I got in some trouble when I was a kid," he stated flatly.

"What kind of trouble?"

He snorted a choked laugh that died almost immediately. "*All* kinds. My folks died in a car wreck when I was eight. Went to live with an aunt and uncle."

"How awful," she whispered.

"They weren't real thrilled with becoming instant parents, so I pretty much raised myself after that."

"But you were just a kid," she said, sympathy for the boy he had been welling within her.

"No, I wasn't," he said quietly, stiffly. "My childhood ended in that car accident."

She could see the tension in his body from across the room. What a lonely life he'd led, she thought sadly. Although her parents hadn't been together, she had always known she was loved. Her gaze moved over Jack and a part of her ached to go to him, ease years-old pain. But Donna knew that he wouldn't appreciate sympathy, so she didn't move. Instead, she held her breath and waited for him to continue.

"Anyway," he said, his voice tight, "the trouble I found escalated the older I got. My aunt and uncle couldn't be bothered to deal with me. So, when I was eighteen, a judge gave me a choice. The corps or jail.''

Donna blinked. She never would have believed that Jack had, at one time, been faced with jail.

He seemed to sense her surprise, or maybe he had simply been ready for it. Turning, he stood straight, shoulders squared, as if someone had planted him against a wall for a firing squad. Not meeting her gaze, he stared straight ahead as he went on. ''Not being a dummy, I chose the corps.'' A sliver of a self-mocking smile tilted one side of his mouth briefly. ''But I almost screwed that up, too.''

''How?'' she whispered, her gaze locked on her husband's stoic, grim features.

''A bad attitude and a big mouth.'' That smile that wasn't a smile chased across his lips again. ''A deadly combination anywhere. But in the corps, a one-way ticket to disaster.''

It was hard to imagine First Sergeant Harris as a big-mouthed private, but she tried.

He rubbed the back of his neck, a sure sign that he wasn't happy. ''Anyway, the colonel—your father—was a lieutenant back then.''

She nodded.

''One day he'd had his fill of my attitude and took me aside for a private lesson in the chain of command.''

Frowning, Donna asked, ''What do you mean?''

''I mean,'' Jack said, looking directly at her for the first time, ''he took off his lieutenant's bars and offered me the chance to back up my mouth with my fists.''

"He *fought* you?''

A different smile briefly appeared on his face then. A smile of admiration. "No, ma'am," he countered. "He beat the hell out of me." At her horrified expression, he added, "In a fair fight."

"I don't believe it," she muttered, trying to imagine her loving, patient father as a brawler.

"Believe it. He convinced me." Jack moved away from the wall and stalked across the small room. "After that," he said while pacing like a caged lion, "he requested me as his radioman. I got to know him. Respect him." He stopped suddenly, his gaze shooting to hers. "He saved my miserable life. I owe him everything."

"So you married his daughter," she said, vaguely surprised that her voice sounded so hollow.

"Yeah."

Ridiculous to feel this pang of disappointment. After all, she'd known that he had only proposed marriage in an attempt to help her father. Why should hearing him say it now affect her in the slightest?

She knew darn well why. Because she had been hoping that maybe he was hiding a small kernel of interest in her. At least now, she knew. That was a good thing, wasn't it?

"Well," she said, deliberately forcing a brightness she didn't feel into her tone, "I guess the debt is paid in full now, huh?"

"I'll never be able to repay him completely," Jack assured her stiffly.

"Jeez, Jack, why don't you just offer to throw yourself on a grenade?" she snapped as a headache leaped into life.

"What?"

"It would be quicker and a lot less painful than having to pretend to love me. To like being married to me." Shut up, she thought. Close your mouth and leave the room. But her feet wouldn't cooperate. She wished she could say the same for her mouth.

"How much of your life are you willing to lay down on the altar of Colonel Thomas Candello?" she asked tightly.

"What the hell are you so mad about?" he demanded.

"I don't know," she shouted right back, throwing her hands high in the air. "I guess, even knowing why we got married, I just don't like the idea of being the poison pill you were forced to swallow for the good of your country."

"What's that supposed to mean?"

"You know," she snapped, "'Close your eyes and think of England.'"

"Huh?"

"You figure it out," she told him as the headache between her eyes began to throb with an insistent, ugly regularity.

"Donna."

"No." She held up one hand, effectively silencing him. "It's okay. I only gave up my apartment, my job, and my roommate. *You* sacrificed your life for the good of your commanding officer."

He took a step closer, but she backed up.

"I'm sure my father appreciates your loyal service, Marine."

"This is nuts," he told her. "Why are we fighting about this now?"

She laughed, more at herself than anything else. "I guess the honeymoon's over, First Sergeant."

"We've been getting along all right so far, haven't we?" Jack asked, apparently determined to smooth things over. Though she couldn't imagine why.

What possible difference could it make now?

"Sure," she said, shrugging in what she hoped conveyed nonchalance.

"Then why can't we just leave it at that?"

"Because we're people, Jack. People talk. People fight."

"What's the point?"

She drew her head back and stared at him as if he'd slapped her. Emotionally, he had. Heck, he wasn't even willing to *fight* with her. She wasn't worth a good argument. "You're right. This whole situation is only temporary. What *is* the point?"

"That's not what I meant."

"Maybe not, but it's the truth."

"Donna—"

Jack looked hard at her and tried to figure out where this had all gone wrong. He'd thought he was giving her what she wanted. A small enough piece of his past to prove to her that they didn't belong together. The reasons behind his loyalty to her father.

Hell, he'd had no idea she would react this way. If he didn't know better, he'd swear she looked as if she were about to cry or something. Over *him?*

That didn't make sense at all.

"What are you so mad about?" he asked finally.

She shook her head slowly. "I'm not mad," she said, but her tone was unconvincing. "I'm just…tired."

Okay, that he understood. He hadn't had a good night's sleep since they'd started sharing a bed. Hoping to help, he offered, "Look, I'll sleep on the couch tonight. Let you get some rest."

She snorted a laugh. "Perfect. You're even willing to sleep on a couch that's two feet too short for you. Heck, Jack, you shouldn't be a marine. You should be a saint."

Anger began to simmer in the pit of his stomach, boiling with other, just as strong emotions to blend into a dangerous mixture. "Why don't you just tell me what you want from me, Donna?"

She opened her mouth as if to speak, then shook her head, more firmly this time. "No. I think it's best if we just forget this whole night ever happened. How about that?"

Forget it? He couldn't even make sense of it. But for the sake of peace and because he didn't want to get any deeper into the mess he'd somehow created for himself, he agreed. "Deal."

"Good." She inhaled sharply, unconsciously

drawing his gaze to the swell of her breasts beneath the dark blue T-shirt she wore. "Now. I'm going to bed. Good night, Jack."

"Good night, Donna," he returned as evenly as possible.

She walked away, headed for the bathroom, and he took a deep, unsteady breath. It was going to be a long night. He wasn't sure how many more nights he was going to be able to survive lying beside her and not touching her.

At that thought, he spoke up suddenly. "Did you talk to housing about fixing the ceiling?"

She stopped in the doorway and turned to look at him.

"Yeah," she said tiredly, "for all the good it did me."

"What'd they say?" he asked, even knowing, from long, painful experience, what the answer to his question would be.

"Let's see..." She tilted her head to one side and tapped her chin with the tip of one finger. "I want to get this right. Oh, yeah." She smiled tightly. "'Mrs. Harris,'" she mimicked in a deep, slow, Southern drawl, "'Of course we'll get on out there just as soon as we can. But it could take some time.'" She dragged the word "time" out to be three syllables long.

Naturally, Jack thought. The corps didn't do anything in a hurry. Except go into battle. *Then* everybody snapped to and got their jobs done in record time. But as far as getting repairs made, he'd probably have his next duty assignment before that ceiling got fixed.

Great.

"Anyway," Donna said, her voice deliberately more cheerful than necessary, "the guy told me how fortunate we were that it was just our 'guest' room that had been ruined. So I don't think they're going to be in any big hurry to get to us."

"I suppose not." Absently, Jack wondered if he could figure out how to fix the damn ceiling himself.

"You coming?" Donna asked before heading for the bedroom again.

Not likely, he thought grimly. Out loud, he said only, "In a minute."

"Okay, then, good night." Then she added. "I'm sorry about—"

"Me, too. 'Night." As she left, his chin dropped to his chest. How could she be so relaxed about the very sleeping arrangements that had him walking around like a zombie for lack of rest?

Easy, he told himself. She obviously didn't want him. So, there was the answer to the problem of whether or not to break his own word about sexless marriages. If the bride wasn't interested, the groom really had nowhere to go.

Jack straightened and looked toward the bedroom. He couldn't help wondering just what kind of horrible karmic debt he was paying off.

They each started out on the edges of the mattress. Lying on either side of an invisible but nonetheless impenetrable brick wall.

As always, though, after a few tense minutes, Donna's breathing deepened and the first, soft sound of humming reached him.

Jack turned his head to look at his wife. Black hair fanned across the pillow, her expression unguarded, Donna's lips curved slightly as if she were enjoying a dream. Well, he was glad one of them had something to smile about.

Donna lay on her side, facing him, one hand stretched out across the mattress as if reaching for him in her sleep. He smiled to himself at the idea. Man, she really was something, Jack thought. Strong, gorgeous, intelligent and funny. Not afraid to face him down in an argument, giving as good as she got. Everything he had ever dreamed of finding in a woman.

A wife.

He shifted his gaze to stare at the ceiling in the dark. Wouldn't his aunt and uncle laugh at him if they could see him now? They'd always told him he was worthless. That no woman would ever love him.

Oh, yeah, he thought grimly. They'd get a real kick out of knowing that the only way he could get a woman to marry him was by swearing that he wouldn't touch her.

Memories rose up inside him, swirling around his mind until the images twisted together into a blinding mass of remembered pain. He'd tried to make them love him. After his parents had died, he'd done everything he could to show his new family that he was worthy of their love.

But they'd paid no more attention to him than they might a stray hound that had wandered into their home. So, just as an unwanted dog would, he had turned on them. It had been as if there'd been a devil on his shoulder, urging him, guiding him into trouble.

He closed his eyes against the old wounds. That Jack was gone, forgotten as he should be. Things were different now. He'd made his own life. He'd become a man to respect. To admire.

But still, just as his aunt and uncle had predicted so long ago, no one loved him.

Donna suddenly rolled up against him. Before he could ease to one side, she'd draped one arm across his chest and snuggled her head into the hollow of his shoulder.

Jack inhaled sharply. His body hardened instantly. He muffled a groan that might have awakened her, and tried to slip out from beneath her. But she only moved in closer, her soft humming becoming louder as she cuddled against him.

Insistent desire ebbed and was replaced by an emotion so tender, it caught him unaware. Lust gave way to the instinct to protect. To cherish. Briefly, he wondered what it might be like to spend the rest of his life like this. With Donna curled in beside him. An imagination he hadn't been aware of before, suddenly produced images of the two of them together, surrounded by kids and dogs. Happy. Laughing. Loving.

He closed his eyes, letting those visions fill his mind until his soul felt full, complete.

His right arm encircled her shoulders and he turned his head to breathe in the flowery scent of her hair. His heartbeat slowed and though the ache in his groin didn't ease one iota, the rest of his body relaxed and for the first time in his marriage, he slipped into a deep, dream-filled sleep.

"'What's married life like?'" Donna repeated her ex-roommate's question to stall for time. Her fingers tightened around the phone receiver. Swallowing the lump in her throat, she said brightly, "It's great. Why wouldn't it be?"

"You tell me," Kathy said, apparently unconvinced by Donna's answer.

Idly, Donna picked at the layers of paint covering the kitchen windowsill. There were dozens of tiny bumps, as if the wood had gotten cold and gooseflesh had hardened on the surface. Scraping her fingernail across one of the hard nubs, she was surprised when the eggshell-white paint peeled up.

"Donna," Kathy said, "something's going on and you're not talking. Unusual, at best. At worst, frightening."

She grimaced and tugged at the loose piece of paint, hoping to flatten it out somewhat. Instead she peeled up a long strip of rubbery substance. Her eyes widened as she stared at the bare wood where paint used to be.

"There's just nothing to tell, Kat," she assured her friend, while trying to tear off the uneven edges of the multilayered paint strip. Another section tore off in her hand. She smothered a groan and tried again.

"You get married to a guy I've never heard of, want me to send you all of your things *and* quit your job for you, and you say there's nothing to talk about?"

"Uh-huh," Donna muttered, hiding a gasp as another, larger section of paint pulled away from the sill.

"What's he like?"

"Gorgeous," came the immediate response that surprised Donna as much as it did her old roommate.

"Well, well..." Kathy practically purred. "The plot thickens."

"What plot?"

"The one in this little mystery."

"Mystery?" Donna countered. "It's more like a romantic farce."

"Okay," Kathy demanded, impatience simmering over the wire. "Give."

"There's nothing to give. I got married. I'm living on base in a reconstituted Quonset hut, I'm unemployed, and the only married virgin in the free world." Oops. She hadn't meant for that part to slip out.

"What?" Kathy's voice hit an all-time high. "Explain."

"What's to explain?" Donna asked, tearing off yet another strip of paint and adding it to the growing pile in front of her on the table. "My gorgeous husband has no interest in me."

"Bull."

"Thank you," Donna said, touched by the vote of confidence.

"Is he crazy?"

"No, just temporary."

"You're losing me here, Don…"

Donna sighed. She hadn't meant to tell anyone about the bizarre marriage she found herself in, but darn it, she had to talk to *somebody*. While she explained the entire situation, she peeled another strip of paint off the window, this time trying for length.

"That is the dumbest thing I've ever heard," Kathy said when she'd finished.

"I've always been an overachiever," Donna conceded, and grinned when the paint strip went all the way to the top of the window casement before snapping off like an old rubber band.

"What are you going to do?"

"What I've been doing," she said, tossing the strip of paint onto the table.

"Which is?"

"Pretend to be a happy little wife."

"What do you *want* to do?"

There's an easy question. She'd known the answer most of her life. She wanted to have a family. Kids. A nice little house somewhere. Two dogs, maybe a cat. But mostly she wanted a husband who loved her. Who wanted to make love with her.

But right now, all of the above boiled down to a single, overwhelming want. "I want to make love with my husband."

"Ahhh..."

"I mean, I'll never have a better opportunity to lose my virginity crown, will I?"

"True," Kathy agreed. "But if you've waited this long, why not wait until the big moment would be special?"

"It would be," Donna admitted, standing to get a better grip on the next strip of paint.

"Uh-oh," her friend said. "Sounds like love."

"Or a close facsimile." She smiled as the paint tore off in a lovely, straight line.

"I don't buy that," Kathy told her. "You've been in lust before and not given in to temptation. What makes him different?"

Donna stopped, dropped the paint strip to hang like a flag on a windless day and stared silently out the window for a long moment. What made Jack different?

Only everything, she thought.

Gray eyes. Strong face. Gentle hands. That look in his eyes that said he didn't expect her to care for him.

So many little things that she wasn't even sure she could list them all.

"Don—"

His laugh, she thought. That was special. Arguing

with him. My, she did enjoy their arguments. And just being in the same room with him was enough to raise her temperature by at least ten degrees. She smiled to herself, remembering how straight and proud he'd stood in front of the Reverend Thistle. How he'd promised to love, honor and cherish her.

A chill swept up her spine and Donna's smile faded as she slowly came to a stunningly undeniable conclusion. "Ohmigod," she whispered.

"What is it?" Kathy demanded.

Donna sat as her knees weakened and her head began to spin. The answer was so obvious. And so terrifying. How had this happened? she wondered frantically.

"I'm falling in love with him," she said softly.

"You're kidding!" her friend shouted loud enough to be heard from Maryland without benefit of the phone.

"No, I'm not," Donna whined. "I'm in love with the one man I shouldn't be. My husband."

Nine

After making that alarming discovery, Donna kept herself so busy over the next several days that she didn't have time to think about it.

Now as she sat back on her heels in the winter sunshine of a November day in California, she paused briefly to admire the bed of impatiens she'd just planted between the two still-straggly bushes beneath the living room window. Then she turned her head to take in the rest of the front yard.

Amazing what a lawnmower and regular watering could do for a place, she told herself. Not to mention the regimentally straight row of petunias aligning the front walk. Idly, she wondered what sorts of flowers the previous owners had planted. There was no way to be sure, since, true to marine tradition, once a family moved out of base housing, the neighbors came in and pillaged the flora—digging up whatever plants weren't original to the house and replanting them in their own yards.

While her mind was busy elsewhere, she didn't even notice Jack's truck pull up in front of the house. He was halfway up the walk when he asked, "Day-dreaming?"

Donna jumped, clutched at her chest as if trying to hold her heart in place, and looked up at him. "You scared me."

He squatted beside her. "I have that effect on a lot of people."

Yeah, but he probably didn't affect many others the way he did her at this particular moment, Donna thought as a familiar, fluttering sensation started up in her stomach.

"Thought you'd be getting ready for your father's party."

She groaned inwardly. There was no way to avoid the small reception Tom Candello had arranged for his daughter and her new husband. When she'd tried to remind her dad that the whole marriage was a temporary situation, he'd insisted that they do every-thing they could to convince everyone that it was a real marriage in every sense.

Hard to argue with that. Though heaven knew, she'd wanted to try. She just didn't want to have to spend hours at her father's house pretending to the world that she loved her husband—while at the same time, pretending to him that she didn't.

"Looks nice," Jack said suddenly, snapping her attention back to him. She looked at him in time to see his gaze sweep across the yard.

"Thanks."

"Why are you doing it?" He turned his head to look at her, his gaze colliding with hers.

"Doing what, exactly?"

"This." He waved one hand at the greenery and the splashes of color.

"I like flowers?" she asked.

"No, I mean..." He shook his head. "I guess I mean that I never figured you for the Mother Earth type."

Intriguing. "And what type *did* you figure me for?"

"I don't know. Luncheons. Fund-raisers. That sort of thing."

Dusting her grubby hands together, Donna folded them in her denim-clad lap, tilted her head to one side and very patiently asked, "What gave you that idea?"

He smiled and Donna's stomach turned completely over. At least, she thought it was her stomach. It might have been her heart. "I don't know, really. But planting flowers, stripping the wood in the house and refinishing it yourself..."

She cleared her throat uneasily and pushed herself to her feet. Well, she'd had to tell him *something* to explain why she'd peeled layer after layer of perfectly good paint off a windowsill.

"Since I remain unemployed," she said, following

him with her gaze as he stood beside her, "I prefer to keep busy."

"That reminds me." Jack reached into the pocket of his camouflage uniform, pulled out a small piece of paper, and handed it to her.

Donna glanced at it. *Marie Talbot, 555-8776.* Lifting her gaze to his again, she asked, "What's this for?"

"She's a teacher at the base school." He smiled at her. "When she found out that you're a sign language interpreter, she asked me to give you her number. Said she could really use someone like you."

He'd found her a job? "And how did she hear about me in the first place?"

He rubbed the back of his neck and let his gaze slide from hers to focus on the new bed of impatiens. "I might have mentioned you to her."

A warm, curl of pleasure snaked through her. He'd been talking about her to other people. Thinking about her. He'd found her a *job.* Giving in to an undeniable impulse, Donna threw herself at him, wrapped her arms around his neck and squeezed, hard. Gazing up at him, she grinned. "You, First Sergeant, are one terrific husband."

His arms closed around her slowly, hesitantly. The restrained strength of his hug took her breath away as he pulled her tightly to him. Her hardened nipples tingled and a like sensation began to burn in the very core of her.

His gaze moved over her features lovingly, as if committing everything about her to memory. When he spoke again, his voice sounded strangled and so soft, she had to strain to hear him at all. "Am I?"

Something in his eyes, a glint of vulnerability, a hint of uncertainty, tore at her. She swallowed the knot of emotion in her throat and rose up onto her toes. Giving in to yet another impulse and unsure of his reaction, she very carefully, very deliberately, kissed him. Beneath her lips, she felt his mouth tighten, then slowly relax.

Nervous and so very hungry for the feel of him, Donna pulled in closer to him, giving herself over to the *rightness* of kissing Jack Harris.

When he groaned from deep in his chest and squeezed her so hard she thought her ribs might crack, she knew she'd reached him. Then he took control of their kiss.

He parted her lips with his tongue, taking her soft exhale of breath into his own lungs. He tasted her, stroked her, caressed her warmth until Donna's knees buckled and only the strength of his arms kept her upright.

Bright splashes of color flashed in front of her closed eyes. She felt as though sparklers were going off in her bloodstream. Though technically still a virgin, she hadn't exactly lived in a closet for twenty-eight years. She'd been kissed before. By men she would have classified as experts.

But *nothing* in her life had prepared her for this.

Explosions of desire rocketed through her. That indescribable ache she'd become accustomed to living with blossomed into a throbbing, demanding need. Her lungs strained for air but she was too busy to breathe. Her hands fisted on his shoulders, her fingers clutching at him.

This kiss was every romance novel she'd ever read, every late-night fantasy she'd ever entertained, and every dream she'd ever held in a safe, dark corner of her heart.

At last, when she was about to faint for lack of air and had ceased to care, he pulled his head back, breaking the almost-magical connection that had bound them so completely to each other.

For a long moment their labored breathing was the only sounds she heard. The scent of a neighbor's barbecue drifted toward them and a cool wind wrapped itself around them, tugging at their clothing.

"Donna," Jack finally whispered, and his eyes shimmered with...regret.

Her mouth still tingling, her knees liquified permanently, she shook her head. She didn't want to hear it. She didn't want what had been an earth-shattering moment for her splintered by the sounds of "I'm sorry." Speaking up quickly, to stop him, she said, "So help me, if you apologize, I'll have you killed."

A slow, sexy smile curved his lips. The shadows left his gray eyes and they shone with amazing clarity. "You're a colonel's daughter. You could probably do it."

One hand slid from his shoulder to cup his cheek. Her thumb traced the high, defined ridge of his cheekbone as she said, "And don't you forget it, mister."

Jack wandered around the colonel's immaculately tended backyard, sticking to the edges of the crowd. His gaze moved over all of the familiar faces. Dozens of people had turned out to attend a spur of the moment barbecue in celebration of Donna's and his marriage.

The sizzle of steaks on the grill whispered above the drone of conversation. A soft breeze lifted the scent of mesquite into the air.

Jack's fingers tightened around the neck of the cold bottle of beer he held as he took a long drink. Elsewhere in the country, people were battening down the hatches, already fighting off winter's cold grip. But in California, it was picnic weather.

As he walked past tight knots of people, his friends slapped him on the back and offered congratulations, while their wives sighed and smiled over the romance of it all.

Romance. He wondered what they'd all think if they knew the truth. Jack took another long pull at his beer. But it didn't do any good. He could still taste Donna. His jaw clenched at the memory that had been dogging him all afternoon. She'd fit into the circle of his arms as if made to be there.

And ever since he had released her, he'd felt empty.

When a master sergeant grabbed his arm and dragged him into a conversation, he went along, although he didn't hear a word any one was saying. Instead he looked for Donna. His wife.

Though there were no ranks visible—everyone was wearing civvies—invisible lines were drawn through the crowd anyway. It happened all the time. The noncommissioned officers and the enlisted men on one side—the officers on the other. And never the twain shall meet.

It was in the midst of the officers' wives that Jack finally located Donna. Her chin-length black hair shining in the afternoon sunshine, she wore a dark red T-shirt tucked into faded blue jeans that hugged her legs as he had dreamed of doing.

"Where's the bride, Harris?" someone close by asked.

Without taking his gaze off her, Jack nodded his head in her direction.

The man beside him grunted. "Well, she *is* a colonel's daughter. Guess it's only right that she hang with the officers."

True. Jack understood. He told himself that it made sense for her to talk to the people she knew. But that did nothing to the twinge of regret that pierced him. This was just another symbol of the differences between them. He was one side of the yard. She was the other.

Donna smiled at the captain's wife and tried to listen to Lieutenant Jorgensen's wife at the same time. But unerringly, her gaze kept drifting across the yard to Jack.

She'd tried, when they first arrived, to meet some

of the enlisted men's spouses. But it was hard. She was so used to playing the role of the colonel's daughter and hostess at his parties, that she wasn't quite sure how to negotiate new waters.

She spotted him then, surrounded by his friends, and felt her heartbeat stagger slightly. In his marine green T-shirt and well-worn Levi's, he looked hard and strong and completely unignorable. But then she'd given up on ignoring him anyway. She figured it was pointless now, since she could still feel the kiss they'd shared.

"Donna?" someone asked. "You okay?"

"Yeah," she answered, keeping her gaze locked on Jack. "I'm fine."

Or, she would be as soon as she made her stand, she told herself. Ever since arriving at the party, she'd been torn between the old Donna and the new—if temporary—one. Should she be the colonel's daughter or the sergeant's wife?

Now, suddenly, she knew the answer and was disgusted with herself that it had taken her so long to realize it.

Suiting actions to the thought, she muttered, "Excuse me," to the ladies and started for her husband.

Jack had seen the indecision on her face. He'd been able to tell, even from across the yard that she wasn't sure what she was supposed to be doing. How to act. He knew his life would be a hell of a lot simpler if she simply stayed where she belonged. With the officers and their families. But, damn it, sometimes simpler wasn't better.

As she left the group of women and started toward him, a determined smile on her face, he felt a bright flash of pride and...*pleasure*. Maybe it was just for show, he told himself. Maybe it was all part of the plan they'd agreed on, to look like the happily married couple. But maybe, he found himself hoping, it was something more.

"Hi, First Sergeant," she said as she came up alongside him.

"Hi, yourself."

"Congratulations," someone said as Jack's friends melted away into the crowd, leaving the two of them alone.

"I didn't mean to scare everyone off," she said, looking after them for a minute before shifting her gaze to his.

He grinned briefly, unable to contain it. "They're marines," he told her in a whisper. "They don't scare."

She smiled and nodded. "Ah, yes, a strategic retreat, then?"

"Much better." God, she was beautiful. His gaze locked on her mouth and it was all he could do not to kiss her senseless in front of her father and everyone else in the yard.

"Hope you don't mind if I hang out with you for a while," she said, her voice carrying a twinge of doubt.

Mind? Hell, at the moment, he wanted to shout. For whatever reason, she'd chosen to come to him rather than stay with her father's friends.

"I think I can stand it," he said in the biggest understatement he'd ever made.

One dark eyebrow arched high on her forehead. She pointed at his beer. "And do you think you might find another one of those, too?"

"Lady," he said, feeling suddenly, inexplicably happy, "I can find anything. I used to be Recon."

"Then get busy, Marine," she said quietly, and moved in close to him.

"Yes, ma'am." He draped his left arm around her shoulders and pulled her tightly to his side. He didn't even ask himself if it was for the benefit of everyone there—or if it was because he couldn't stand not touching her for another minute.

The reasons no longer mattered to him. All that counted now was holding her.

Tom Candello looked past the crowd to where his daughter and her husband stood staring into each other's eyes. A swell of pleasure rushed through him. Maybe it would all work out, he thought. Maybe the two of them would realize how good they could be together.

He'd seen his daughter hurt and humiliated by the wrong man. Now he'd like to see her find love with a man he knew would be good to her.

"What are you thinking?" A woman walked up beside him, dragging his attention away from Donna and Jack.

"Hmm?" He swiveled his head and caught himself smiling. Major Sally Taylor. Dedicated career

officer, brilliant mind—and God help him, great legs.
He scratched that thought immediately. A man
couldn't be too careful these days.

"Oh," he said at last, after noticing the patient
expression on her face, "I was just thinking what a
nice-looking couple they make."

She followed his gaze and nodded. "Yes, they do.
I hope everything works out well for them."

"You don't sound hopeful," he commented, re-
acting to the cynical note in her voice.

Sally chuckled and shook her head. "That's because I'm not, Colonel."

"We're off duty," he reminded her, "Call me
Tom."

"All right, Tom. I'm Sally."

"Now that we have that settled," he said, glad to
at least be on a first name-basis at last, "why so
cynical?"

She lifted her glass of iced tea and took a sip before saying, "Because I'm all grown up now, Tom.
And fairy-tale endings are for kids."

He blinked, not sure what to say to that. She
smiled and moved off to talk to Lieutenant Jorgensen.

The sky was blanketed with stars when Jack and
Donna started for home. With soft jazz pouring from
the truck's CD player, they drove through the base
slowly, as if neither of them was in any particular
hurry to get home.

"Who was that woman talking to my father most

of the night?'' she asked finally, more to end the silence than anything else.

"Major Taylor,'' Jack said shortly. "She's new here. Hasn't been on Pendleton for more than a month or so.''

"Dad sure seems interested in her.''

"Does that bother you?'' he asked, glancing at her briefly.

"I don't know,'' she admitted, not at all sure if she was comfortable with the idea of her father actually dating someone. It didn't matter if he was fairly young and handsome. Or even that he'd been alone for most of his life. It was just an odd sensation, thinking of your parents as having a private life. A love life. "I guess it feels a little strange,'' she said, "but I hope everything works out for him.'' Better, she added silently, than things had been working out for *her*.

Another minute or two of silence spun out before Jack said softly. "It was a nice party.''

"Yes, it was.''

"Everyone seemed to have a good time.''

"Seemed to,'' she agreed.

"Did you?'' he asked, glancing at her again.

Donna took a long moment before answering. She studied his profile in the dim, reflected glow of the dash lights. Strong, rugged, and completely, heart-stoppingly attractive.

When had this marriage stopped being a pretense to her? When had she begun to care for this man? And did it really matter?

"Yes," she said finally. "I did."

He shifted another look at her and gave her a small smile. "Me, too."

In another moment he was pulling up in front of their house and cutting the engine. When he shut off the headlights, dark fell down around them like a thick, new blanket.

Giving in to an impulse, Donna quickly unhooked her seat belt and slid across the bench seat toward him.

Jack inhaled sharply, half turning his head toward her. "Donna—"

"Jack." She lifted one hand to cover his mouth with her fingertips. "Don't say anything, okay?"

He caught her hand with his and said quietly, "I just don't think—"

"Good," she interrupted again. "Maybe it's time we both stopped thinking and started feeling."

Then she leaned in, tilted her head and kissed him.

After an instant's hesitation, he kissed her right back. As if picking up where they'd left off, passion burst into life, igniting the inside of the small pickup like a match set to gasoline.

Jack groaned and grabbed her to him, shifting in the seat to drag her across his lap. She wiggled her bottom, looking for a comfortable position, and unknowingly, torturing him further. His groin hard and ready, as it had been during each of the long, frustrating nights of their marriage, he groaned from the back of his throat as she settled in his lap.

She reached up, cupped his face with her hands

and deepened their kiss. He parted her lips with his tongue and plundered her with all of the thoroughness of a marine landing in enemy territory.

Donna moaned gently and pressed her breasts against his chest. Even through the fabric of their shirts and the confinement of her bra, he felt the rigid tips of her nipples and had to touch them. Caress them. Taste them.

He pulled her T-shirt free of the waistband of her jeans and slid his hands up over the smooth, warm skin of her back. In seconds he had her bra clasp undone. His left hand skimmed around to cup one breast and his thumb rubbed her nipple until she arched into him, instinctively seeking more.

Reluctantly, he broke the kiss and bent his head to take that small, hard bud into his mouth. He felt her fingers cup the back of his head, holding him to her. And when he suckled her, she gasped and let her head fall back on her neck.

"Oh, Jack..." she whispered brokenly.

His lips and teeth teased her sensitive flesh until he was crazy with want and need. His body felt as though it was about to explode, and every one of her quick intakes of breath only fanned flames that were threatening to engulf him completely.

Her hands moved to his shoulders, her fingers clutching at him, digging into his skin through the fabric of his T-shirt. Her hips bucked on his lap, she could feel that he was as hard as steel.

"Donna," he whispered as he lifted his head for

another kiss, "I have to touch you. Feel you. All of you."

"Yes, Jack," she answered, her words tumbling from her in a rush. "I need that, too. Now. Please, now."

Already, his fingers were working at the button and zipper of her jeans. She twisted in his arms, trying to help but succeeding only in torturing him further.

At last the brass button popped free and the zipper slid down noiselessly, allowing him access to her body. To the secrets he'd been wanting to delve ever since that first night when he'd rescued her and then lain awake all night staring at her.

Sliding his fingers beneath the fragile elastic of her bikini underwear, he pushed onward, downward, until he felt the soft brush of curls covering her most intimate flesh.

She gasped again, louder this time, and lifted her hips slightly into his touch.

His heartbeat slowed, then seemed to stop altogether when he touched her damp heat for the first time. She sucked in a gulp of air and wiggled her hips, inviting him, silently asking him to explore her body.

His fingertips skimmed across the small, sensitive nub of flesh at the peak of her center and she shuddered in his arms. His left arm tightened around her, holding her securely while his right hand sent her spiraling out of control.

Fighting against the confines of the denim jeans,

he dipped one finger into her liquid heat and sighed in satisfaction when she groaned.

It wasn't enough, he thought desperately. Not nearly enough. He wanted to have her naked beneath him. Open to his entry. He wanted to push his body into hers and feel her quivering response. He wanted to watch her reach that ultimate feeling of ecstasy just before emptying himself within her.

"Jack," she whispered, and shifted her hips again. "This feels…"

"Too confining?" he asked quietly, and leaned forward to press a kiss to the pulse point in her throat.

"Wonderful," she finished, and arched into his hand again.

"Let's go inside, Donna," he said, wanting to move now, while he could still walk.

"It's too far away," she argued.

"We need more room, Donna," he told her, reluctantly pulling his hand free of her jeans.

She groaned her disappointment, but lifted her head to look at him. "Room?" she repeated.

"To romp," he told her, already reaching for the door handle.

Ten

The short walk to the front door had never seemed so long before. They practically raced each other to the house.

Once inside, with the door closed and locked, they fell together, lips seeking, hands grasping. In a hushed symphony of whispered urgency, they stumbled across the living room to the bedroom where they had lain together yet apart since their marriage.

Tumbling down onto the mattress, Jack propped himself up on one elbow, staring down into her face as though he needed reassurance from her that she really did want him. One hand slid under the front of her T-shirt, then beneath her still-loosened bra to cup one of her breasts. As his fingers smoothed across her hardened nipple, she gasped, arching her back like a kitten demanding to be stroked.

"Donna," he asked quietly, "are you sure you want this?"

"Look at me," she answered, a soft, strained smile on her face. "My heart's racing, my legs couldn't support me if I tried to walk, and every time you touch me, I forget to breathe."

His throat tightened unexpectedly. Emotion rose up in him. Emotions that terrified him, yet filled him with pleasure.

His thumb caressed her nipple and she squeezed her eyes shut briefly.

"Yeah, Jack. I'm sure."

"Thank God," he murmured, and bent his head to claim a kiss. His lips brushed across hers gently. His teeth nipped at her lower lip and his tongue defined the shape of her mouth before slipping into her warmth and stoking the fires within into an inferno.

He tugged the hem of her shirt up and pushed the fine white lace bra aside. Breaking the kiss, Jack inhaled sharply and filled his gaze with the sight of the smooth, creamy flesh he'd dreamed of caressing. As he dragged the palm of his hand lightly across her chest, he felt her heartbeat thundering behind her rib cage.

He swallowed heavily and his own heartbeat jumped into a matching rhythm. Dipping his head, he claimed first one nipple, then the other, flicking at the dark, rosy buds with the tip of his tongue until Donna twisted and writhed beneath him.

Her hands bunched in the fabric of his shirt and when she tried to pull it up so that she could caress his skin, he sat up, pulling her with him. "Too many clothes here," he whispered, and gently lifted her shirt up and over her head.

"Way too many," she agreed, reaching for the hem of his shirt, tugging it off, and tossing it to the floor.

He eased her bra straps down off her shoulders and along her arms until it, too, landed in a heap on the floor.

In seconds she was in his arms again, and the incredible sensation of his skin brushing against hers pushed him over the fine line he'd been walking.

Without words, they tore the rest of their clothing off, and turned to each other in a haze of desire so intense neither of them could have spoken if they'd tried. But there was no need for words. Not now. Now, there was only the need to touch. Taste. Discover.

Impatiently yanking the multicolored quilt off, Jack laid Donna down on the cool, flower-sprigged cotton sheets and leaned over her. He kissed her until his lungs were clamoring for air, and still he didn't want to stop. But there was so much more he wanted to do to her. With her. Tearing his mouth free of hers, he slid his lips along the line of her jaw to the column of her neck. His tongue traced a warm, damp course down the elegant column and he paused at the base of her throat to test the thrumming pulse point hidden there.

She moved against him, arching, twisting, holding his head to her as if afraid he would stop. As his mouth tormented her, his hands slid over her body, discovering and exploring every dip, every curve. His calloused fingertips stroked her satiny skin with the delicate touch of a sculptor working with glass. Yet the hunger, the need, continued to build until he felt as though he could never feel enough of her…taste enough of her.

At last, his right hand skimmed over the curve of her hip and along her thigh. Caressing the inner flesh of her leg, his fingers dusted across her center in a promise of things to come.

She jerked in his arms and tipped her head back into the mattress. Her legs parted for him and he accepted her invitation. As his hand cupped her warmth, she shivered, her hips lifting from the bed, moving into his hand, instinctively searching for the completion they both needed so badly.

Raising his head, he stared down into her passion-glazed eyes, wanting to remember every second of this time with her. Every moment. He wasn't fool enough to think that this changed anything. That she would be with him forever. But that knowledge only made tonight more special. More wondrous. And in the years to come, he knew he would turn to this memory often.

Threads of moonlight pierced the room, sliding through the gaps in the curtains. Her lips parted as puffs of strangled breath escaped her lungs. A soft, cold breeze slipped beneath the partly opened window, scattering gooseflesh over her body.

"Cold?" he whispered.

She shook her head. "Not enough to stop to close the window." Cupping his face with one hand, she smoothed her fingertips across his cheekbone, sending spears of light and heat deep into the darkest corners of his soul. Corners he had been sure were closed off forever.

Any danger warnings coming from the back of his mind, though, were ignored. He couldn't have walked away from this woman if his life had depended on it.

Breathlessly, he slipped one finger into her passage, eager now to become a part of her. To touch her as deeply as she had him.

So tight, so warm. His heartbeat thundered in his ears as he stroked her inner flesh. She planted both feet firmly on the mattress and lifted her hips again and again, rocking with an ancient rhythm, silently pleading with him, demanding everything from him.

Groaning, he surrendered to the moment. Shifting position until he knelt between her updrawn legs, he withdrew his hand from her body despite her moan of disappointment.

Donna fought for a breath she couldn't catch. Every nerve in her body was sizzling with an inner fire so hot and wild, she was afraid it would never be quenched.

This was so much more than she'd ever imagined. Every touch of Jack's hands sent her skittering closer to the edge of a precipice she'd never even been near before.

She looked up at him as he moved to kneel in front of her. His gray eyes glittered in the moonlight. His broad muscular chest tapered to a narrow waist and hips. But it was the hard, solid length of him that made her eyes widen in both desire and apprehension. Ridiculous thing to have to admit at the ripe old age of twenty-eight, but she was a little scared. What if they didn't fit together? What if he was too— she looked again—big? What if she did something wrong and not only ruined her initiation into lovemaking but humiliated herself into the bargain?

What if she was disappointed?

No. What if *he* was disappointed?

Lord. Was it too late to stop? To change her mind? To go to her grave a vestal virgin, untouched by any man?

His fingertips stroked her damp inner flesh again and the throbbing ache centered there tripled. She bit down hard on her bottom lip. Definitely too late to stop. She couldn't back out now. She had to know it all. And most importantly, she wanted Jack Harris to be the man who showed her all of the secrets she'd waited so long to learn. She wanted him to feel for her what she felt for him. She wanted this marriage to be a real one, damn it.

"Jack," she said brokenly, "I want—" Half sitting, she reached for him. He caught her hands, threading his fingers through hers. Still keeping their hands locked together, palm to palm, he loomed over her, bracing their entwined hands on the mattress at either side of her head.

He bent to kiss her briefly and then she felt the soft, hard tip of him as his body searched for the entry to hers. Instinctively she lifted her hips, moving into him, drawing him closer, deeper.

And then he was inside her, slowly pushing himself into her warmth. Her eyes widened at the unfamiliar yet completely wonderful sensation. She felt her body stretch to accommodate his presence and her breath caught in her throat at the utter beauty of the moment. Sweet tears stung the backs of her eyes, but she blinked them away. She didn't want him to see tears and think she was uncomfortable, and she doubted he would believe her if she told him that she was crying because he was simply too beautiful, too wonderful to be real.

The thick, rigid length of him pierced her body with a gentle insistence. She stared up into his eyes and saw him frown slightly, his brow furrowed in concentration.

"So tight," he whispered, bending his head for another brief kiss. "So small and tight."

She choked back a groan of misery. He *was* disappointed. "Is that bad?" she asked.

He smiled ruefully. "Not hardly," he said, and pushed himself all the way inside her.

Donna gasped, then clutched at his hands, still entwined with hers. Her fingernails dug into his flesh.

Jack went completely still, his body buried so deep

within her, she was sure she could feel him touching her heart.

"You're a virgin," he said flatly.

"Not now," she told him with a pleased smile.

"Donna." His head dropped to his chest. "You should have told me."

"Why? Would it have changed things?"

"I don't know. Maybe."

She shook her head. "Then I'm glad I didn't tell you. Because I wouldn't change a thing."

He lifted his head again to stare down at her. Their gazes locked and she tried to tell him with her eyes what she couldn't quite bring herself to say yet. That she loved him. That she wanted him more than her next breath. That she would die if he pulled away from her now.

She twisted her hips slightly as her discomfort eased and he sucked in a gulp of air at her movement. Smiling to herself, she repeated the maneuver and Jack's eyes closed.

"Jack," she whispered. "Don't stop. Please don't stop."

His eyes opened again and he looked down at her. "I won't stop, Donna. I won't ever stop."

Then he moved, rocking his hips against her, and the friction of that movement sent new tremors of expectation racing along her spine. She moaned gently, arching her head back into the mattress. Trying to mimic his actions, her hips moved, too, with him, into him, driving them both onward, pushing them toward the edge of completion that waited, shimmering, just out of reach.

Her heartbeat staggered. Her chest heaved with the effort to breathe. And none of it mattered. Every thought in her head was centered on the exquisite sensations rocketing through her body.

Jack set the rhythm of their dance and Donna matched him move for move. When at last he freed one of his hands and skimmed it down between their bodies, she was desperate with need. So completely caught in a web of passion and desire that she felt as though she would never be able to draw an easy breath again.

Then he touched her. His fingertips stroked one small, incredibly sensitive piece of flesh and stars exploded in the room. Her body jerked. Her legs locked around his hips, holding him to her. She shouted his name as tremors coursed through her limbs, making her feel both weak and energized at the same time.

A heartbeat later Jack's body stiffened, he threw his head back and, groaning her name, joined her in the sweet rush of fulfillment.

He collapsed on top of her and Donna smoothed her hands up and down his back, relishing the strong, warm feel of his flesh. His heavy weight felt comforting, right somehow. When he tried to roll off of her, she held him still. "No," she said softly. "Stay with me awhile longer."

"I'm too heavy," he argued, lifting his head to look down at her.

"No, you're not." She smiled and boldly slid her hands farther down his back to the curve of his rear. She explored his body with the same tender thoroughness that he had hers and watched his gray eyes shimmer with a renewed passion.

"Donna," he warned her, "it's too soon. You'll be sore enough as it is."

She shook her head against the sheets. "I want to feel all of it again," she told him, her hands cupping his bottom and kneading his flesh. "And if I'm already sore, why not?"

"You're crazy, you know that?" he asked, dipping his head to plant a kiss at the corner of her mouth.

She turned her face into his, kissing him deeply, fully. Her tongue parted his lips and swept into his mouth, and his teasing manner instantly fell away, dissolving into a fresh storm of rising passion.

Deep within her, Donna felt his body tighten in response to her kiss and she felt the first stirrings of a delicious sense of power. Whatever he may claim to the contrary, Donna knew in that moment that he was far from feeling nothing toward her.

Unlike the first time, there were no soft murmurs, no lazy strokes and caresses. Now there was only a hunger to be fed. A desire to be quenched.

His mouth on hers became ferocious. Nipping with his teeth and grinding his lips against hers, Jack laid claim to her, body and soul. Donna groaned into his mouth and gave herself over to the tumultuous feelings swamping her. Clutching at his back, her fingernails dragged along his spine, as if branding his flesh the way she hoped she was branding his heart.

Drawing her legs up, she locked them tight around his hips, pulling him deeper, harder, inside her. When he began moving within her, she shuddered violently at his strength and gentleness. His hips bucked against hers. She moved into him, knowing now what pleasure awaited her and desperately anxious to experience it again.

Small spirals of delight began to build at her core and she tightened her muscles, straining to reach that starburst of sensation.

His harsh breathing puffed against her ear. She felt the muscles of his back bunch and cord beneath her hands. His powerful thrusts inched her backward on the mattress and she held on to him as though he were the only stable point left in her universe.

And then, almost without warning, that world exploded again. In a bright swirl of color and light, she found not the same completion she had expected, but a deeper, more vibrant, more all-encompassing swell of delight. She rode the wave of pleasure as far as it would take her, and then gathered Jack to her tightly when he cried out, emptying himself into her depths.

Hours later she woke up, cradled in his arms.

Jack held her close when she would have moved, unwilling to give up the feel of her tucked safely beside him.

"Did I fall asleep?" she whispered, her warm

breath brushing across his chest with a feather-light touch.

He chuckled. "No, ma'am," he said, his hands stroking up and down the length of her back. "You fell unconscious."

Despite his tight hold on her, she managed to lift her head to look at him. Tossing her dark hair back out of her eyes, she said, "You shouldn't have let me sleep, Jack. I don't want to miss a minute of this night."

"Honey," he told her, smoothing back that stubborn lock of hair again, "you're new at this, remember? You've had enough for one night."

"No." She shook her head, tumbling her dark hair back into her eyes only to be swept aside again. She bent and kissed one of his flat, brown nipples, running her tongue across the pebbly surface.

He groaned as the sensation of her tongue on him swept down throughout his body. Amazing, he thought, but he was ready and raring to go. Again. It seemed that he couldn't get enough of this incredible woman. And maybe, at least for this one night, he shouldn't think beyond that thought.

There would be time enough for thinking in the morning. And the morning after that. Something inside him coiled tight and dark as he realized that very soon she would probably regret every moment they had shared in this tiny room. Shouldn't he take the opportunity to build enough memories to see him through the lonely years he would face without her?

"Donna…"

She smiled and lifted her head again. "I've waited a long time for this, Jack. I don't want to wait another minute."

"Baby," he said reluctantly, "if we go again this soon, you won't be able to walk tomorrow."

"Then we'll spend the day in bed." Her eyebrows wiggled and her smile broadened just a bit.

"Man, whatever happened to shy virgins?" he asked, though he was infinitely grateful that she obviously wanted him as badly as he did her.

"It's a myth," she told him, bending to taste that flat nipple of his again. The tip of her tongue traced across that piece of sensitive flesh and Jack's arm around her tightened further. Lifting her head again, she looked at him out of one eye. "Virgins aren't shy. They just don't know what they're missing. Once we find out—there's no stopping us."

"I'm convinced," he muttered thickly as her right hand began to stroke his belly and parts farther south.

"You know, Jack," she whispered between hasty kisses following the narrow trail of curls down the length of his chest, "I really think I'm getting the hang of this. There's really not a lot to learn, is there?"

He caught her head in his hands and brought her face to his. Sealing her lips closed with a mind-boggling kiss, he finally let her go long enough to assure her. "Baby, this class is just getting started. You're a *long* way from graduating."

Then, before she could say a word, Jack flipped her onto her back.

"Hey! What are you doing?"

"You'll find out," he said, his voice low and husky, filled with promises of long nights and careful loving.

"Jack..."

She reached for him but he pushed her hands aside then dipped his head to claim first one hard, rigid nipple then the other. Slowly, lavishly, he worshiped them, each in turn. His tongue swirled around the dark, pebbly buds and he nibbled at her with the edges of his teeth.

He felt her passion blossom beneath his touch. Pleasure tore through him as he realized that for the first time in his life, giving satisfaction was more important to him than finding it himself.

His hands swept up and down the length of her, his fingertips sliding into her warmth and then out again, leaving her breathless and tortured. She tossed her head from side to side on the pillow and small, inarticulate sounds erupted from her throat.

He smiled and slowly trailed kisses down her rib cage, across her abdomen and past the triangle of dark curls that hid her treasures from him.

She flinched and tried to move away. "Jack, what are you doing?"

He held her still, his big hands gentle but firm on her hips as he moved to kneel between her legs. Glancing into her eyes, he smiled and said, "I'm keeping you after school for an extra lesson."

"Jack—" She shook her head, one hand reaching toward him. "I don't think—"

"Good." He cut her off neatly. "Don't think. Feel."

Lifting her bottom from the mattress, he held her, suspended as he nudged first one of her legs, then the other, over his shoulders.

Her hands fisted in the sheets and her eyes held a glimmer of wary apprehension. Then his mouth covered her and she whimpered helplessly.

Jack sipped at her as though her body was a cup, containing the finest, most intoxicating brew. With his tongue, he stroked her most sensitive spot until she was trembling in his arms. Glancing at her again, he saw her eyes close as she trustingly gave herself to him, opening herself to whatever he chose to do to her—with her.

Her surrender fed his own passion and he deepened his touch, sliding one finger into her depths as he continued to lavish attention on her inner flesh.

Donna gasped, opened her eyes and looked at the man she loved as he caressed her more intimately than she had thought possible. She should be embarrassed, she knew. At the very least, she should close her eyes so that she wouldn't have to *see* what he was doing to her.

But she couldn't. Her gaze locked on him as her heartbeat accelerated until she thought it would burst from her chest. Intense spears of delight shot through her body, ricocheting off of each other until she was nothing more than a coil of anticipation, being wound tighter and tighter with every passing moment.

He stroked her with his tongue again and suckled gently at a spot that seemed to be directly linked to every nerve in her body. Tremors coursed through her. She heard herself whimper again and was powerless to stop it. As an internal tension built she was certain would kill her with its strength, she reached forward and cupped the back of his head, holding him to her.

And when the first incredible shudder shot through her, she held him tightly to her. She shouted, "Jack!" as her body exploded in his arms and kept him firmly locked to her until the last, lingering ripples of satisfaction faded away.

Finally spent, her hands fell to her sides and she lay limply in his strong hands. When she gathered the strength to open her eyes, she looked up and met his desire-filled gaze.

She didn't know what to say. What *could* she say to a man who had just done what he had?

Thankfully, Jack solved that problem for her. He gently set her back onto the bed, smiled and whispered, "Class dismissed."

Eleven

After a couple of hours of sleep, they awoke to the slivers of dawn poking through the gaps in the curtains.

Donna moaned quietly and stretched against him.

Jack's teeth ground together as he tried to halt his body's instantaneous reaction. But that, as he realized a moment later, was a losing battle. It seemed all she had to do was draw a breath and he was eager to become a part of her again. To feel her warmth surround him, pulling him inside her, where he wasn't alone. Where incredibly, after all of these lonely years, he had found peace.

But it was a temporary contentment and he knew it. As if to remind himself of that fact, he swung his legs off the bed and stood.

"Where you going?" she murmured, her voice still husky, whether from sleep or renewed passion he didn't know—and couldn't afford to find out.

"Take a shower," he said abruptly. "Gotta get to work."

She pushed herself into a sitting position and the sheet dropped away, puddling in her lap. Instantly his gaze dropped to the swell of her breasts and his palms itched to cup them, caress them.

He inhaled sharply and told himself to get a grip.

Donna raked one hand through her tousled hair, shoving it back from her face with lazy grace. Slanting him a smile, she yawned, then said, "I guess I'd better get moving, too. Talk to Marie Talbot about that job."

He nodded but couldn't help wondering if she would be telling Ms. Talbot that she would only be on base temporarily. Or would she keep it a secret, continuing the charade of their marriage?

A marriage that, for last night anyway, had felt suddenly, and completely, real. Memories filled him, rushing through his mind like a strong gust of sea air. Images of her, open and trusting, reaching for him, crying his name, rose up in his brain and he wondered how he would ever live without her.

She absently rubbed her stomach as it grumbled noisily.

"Guess I worked up an appetite," she said, and gingerly moved to the edge of the bed.

"Sore?" he asked, even knowing the answer.

She shot him a quick, mischievous look. "It was worth it."

Like a bolt of lightning, sudden realization struck him with the force of a blow that threatened to knock him to his knees. She'd been a virgin. Jack's eyes widened as the implications of that fact raced home.

How stupid could one man be? he wondered frantically. Desire was no excuse. Passion no defense. He could only hope that she had been smarter than he.

Warily he asked, "Donna?"

"Uh-huh?" She eased up off the bed and stood facing him, naked and completely unselfconscious.

"I'm ashamed to admit it, but something only just now occurred to me."

"What's that?" she asked, taking a step toward him as if to comfort him.

"Last night..." he said, holding up one hand to ward her off long enough to let him keep his thoughts straight. "Please tell me you were safe."

She laughed and he felt a momentary respite from the worry that had suddenly dropped over him like an early morning fog.

"Of course, I'm safe," she told him. "That's one good thing about a virgin, Jack. No worry about diseases." She paled then and looked at him. "You're not—"

"No," he assured her quickly. "I'm healthy. I'm not talking about diseases here, Donna. I'm trying to ask you if you're on the Pill."

She laughed again.

Incredible.

"Now why would a *virgin* be on the Pill?" she said, smiling and shaking her head at the notion.

The sinking sensation in the pit of his stomach was apparently contagious. He watched her face pale again and when she plopped down onto the bed behind her, he wasn't even surprised at her stunned expression. "Ohmigod," she whispered.

"You can say that again," he muttered as his temporary marriage suddenly began to look a lot more permanent.

All day Donna tried to dismiss the worries from her mind. After all, she told herself, it wouldn't do her a damn bit of good to get all wound up about it. She either was or wasn't pregnant. It was too late now to do anything about the situation one way or the other.

Instead she concentrated on her new job. Marie Talbot, an older woman with gray hair and sparkling green eyes had hired her on the spot and immediately put her to work.

There was only one child in the base school who was hearing impaired. Dylan, a nine-year-old boy, had taken signing courses before, but his skills had weakened since he'd had no one to continue his lessons. The first time Donna signed to him, his eyes lit up with excitement.

And as the day went on, Donna was pleased to note that some of his classmates, intrigued with her flashing hands and Dylan's giggles, wandered over, expressing interest in learning.

Within an hour or so, Dylan was transformed from a shy, solitary child to an excited little boy, eager to make friends and teach them how to talk to him.

Her day flew past and Donna was thankful. It wasn't until she was driving home from work that she at last had time to think about the possible repercussions of her one wild night of lovemaking.

Hands tight on the steering wheel, she let her mind race from one blossoming thought to the next. No matter what happened, she resolved firmly, she wouldn't regret a moment of what she and Jack had shared. Already, those hours with him in the dark had taken on a misty, dreamlike quality, too perfect to be real.

She should have known it was too good to last.

But why couldn't it? she asked herself, stopping at a red light. As a trickle of cars streamed through the intersection, she stared blankly ahead.

Okay, her judgment was lousy. She could accept that. But she hadn't actually *chosen* Jack. Fate had. Surely that counted for something. On the other hand, knowing her judgment was so bad, was loving Jack a good thing? Or a bad thing?

The fact that her father approved of Jack was reassuring. Dad had *never* liked Kyle. Still, she had to admit that Jack had never shown any signs at all of wanting to *stay* married.

Her head hurt. A dull, throbbing headache pulsed

behind her eyes and she leaned forward, resting her head on the cool, black steering wheel of the truck Jack had insisted she drive. Why was her life always so complicated? Why couldn't she do anything like a normal person? Fall in love, then get married, then have a baby?

Oh, no. Donna Candello Harris had to get married, make a baby, then fall in love.

One hand dropped to her flat abdomen on that thought. Was there a baby already growing inside her? She sucked in a gulp of air and told herself that she only had another week or so to find out. She'd always been as regular as clockwork. If she missed her next cycle, then she'd know.

Something warm and lovely settled in the pit of her stomach. Jack's baby. *Their* baby. With her dark hair and his gray eyes. She smiled to herself and squeezed her eyes shut, the better to build an image of her maybe-baby.

And that image was suddenly so strong, she could almost feel her child lying safe in the crook of her arm. She could *see* the proud gleam in Jack's eyes and taste his kiss as he admired his daughter.

Oh, yes, she thought. It would be a girl. A girl who would wrap her daddy around her little finger as easily as she would wrap herself around his heart.

Donna caught herself as her fantasy blossomed to include three more children, a nice house and a flower-filled yard. This was ridiculous. She didn't even know if the man loved her or not. She thought he did, but God knew, she'd been wrong before.

A horn blasted into the silence, startling her.

Donna jerked upright, shot a glance into her rear-view mirror at the irate man waving her on, then looked at the now green light. Obediently, she stepped on the gas.

"So help me," Tom Haley said stiffly, "you bark one more order at me and I'll borrow a tank and turn you into a spot on the road."

Jack glared at his longtime friend as the other man stomped out of their shared office. He couldn't blame Tom. Hell, if he had been in Tom's shoes, Jack would have punched himself senseless.

His frustration had been riding him all day and Tom had just been the most convenient person to dump on.

Jack set both hands on either side of his skull and squeezed, as if he could rid himself of his thoughts and the pounding headache accompanying them. But it didn't help. Visions of Donna still rose up in his brain, blinding him to work, friendship, *everything* else.

What if she was pregnant? What then?

The thought of Donna and him making a child together filled him with warring emotions. Pleasure, first and foremost, followed quickly by desperation and fear.

A helluva thing for a career marine to admit to.

But there it was. Jack rubbed one hand over his tired eyes and sank back into his chair. Staring up at the ceiling, he acknowledged that the coiled tension in his belly could only be fear.

Fear that when she eventually left him—and he didn't have a doubt that she would—he wouldn't be able to go on without her.

For most of his life, the corps had been everything to him. Father, mother, lover, wife. His sense of duty had been polished and honed like the sharpest of steel knives. Honor was as much a part of him as the color of his hair and eyes.

But how could he act in an honorable fashion—sticking to their temporary marriage vows—when everything inside him screamed to never let her go?

"Jack?"

He straightened and jumped to his feet at the sound of that familiar voice. "Colonel, Sir," he said, keeping his gaze from meeting that of his father-in-law's.

"How's everything?"

"Fine, Sir," Jack replied, his features frozen into the stony mask of a full attention stance.

"At ease, first sergeant," the colonel told him.

Jack followed orders. He always followed orders. Finally, unable to avoid it any longer, he looked at the man in the doorway. For years he'd respected and admired Colonel Candello. He'd looked forward to the times when they worked together. When they could talk, man to man.

Now all he could think was that he wished the colonel would go away. Leave him to his misery.

"Just wanted to stop and make sure you and

Donna would be coming to Thanksgiving dinner next week.''

Thanksgiving? Had it only been a few weeks since he'd first laid eyes on Donna? Impossible. It felt as though he'd known her forever.

''Jack?'' the colonel prompted.

He shook himself from his thoughts and focused on the here and now. With no graceful way out of the invitation, he finally snapped, ''Yes, Sir. Thank you, Sir.''

Tom Candello's eyes narrowed slightly as he looked at him, and Jack found himself grateful the other man couldn't read minds.

''If I'm out of line here,'' the colonel said at last, ''feel free to say so. This isn't between a commanding officer and his first sergeant. This is between a father-in-law and his daughter's husband.''

Jack braced himself.

''Is everything all right between you two?''

''Sir?''

''Would it help if I invited myself to dinner? The three of us could spend some time together.'' He paused meaningfully. ''Talk.''

Jack shook his head. ''I don't think so, Sir. Thanks, anyway.''

''Jack,'' the colonel went on, ''I think if you'll just—''

He cut him off, trusting the man had meant what he said about this not being about ranks. ''Beg pardon, Sir, but this is between Donna and me. It'd be best if you back off.''

Tom Candello's eyebrows lifted and he whistled softly, tunelessly. "That bad?"

Jack forced a shrug.

"Okay, Jack." Clearly reluctant to let it go, the colonel nodded. "You two work it out."

"There's nothing to work out, Sir. This was a temporary solution to a problem. That's all." The words sounded phony even to him.

Colonel Candello's features tightened slightly. "I'll butt out, for now. But don't you do anything stupid, Jack. Don't do or say something the two of you might come to regret."

"Sir." Neither an agreement nor a denial.

The colonel shook his head wearily. "I'll let you get back to work," he said, turning in the doorway.

Jack didn't answer. He didn't need to. The colonel was already gone.

That night the strained silence that had hovered between them over dinner, splintered suddenly.

Jack had been walking on eggshells around her, sure that one wrong word from him would send her racing to the airport, eager to get away and end this farce.

But, damn it, at the same time, he'd been torturing himself with thoughts of what might have been. He didn't know if he loved her or not—the way he was raised, he'd never been close enough to love to identify it, much less experience it firsthand.

But he did know that he looked forward to the end of his shift now. He left his desk in a hurry every night, eager to return to this little house where Donna could be found. He liked fighting his way past her panty hose, drying on the rod, to take his morning shower. He liked the smell of her perfume as it seemed to hang in every corner of the house. He liked to watch her push her hair out of her eyes when it got in her way. And making love with her had filled all of the lonely, empty spots inside him.

Even with this terrible, uncomfortable tension between them, there was nowhere he'd rather be.

And he liked the way she hummed in her sleep.

But he couldn't live on the edge like this. Waiting for her to leave would kill him slowly. Much better to go out with a bomb blast and get it over with all at once.

"About Thanksgiving dinner at your father's house," he said.

"What about it?"

She kept her gaze locked on her dinner plate. The pot roast was good, but it wasn't *that* good. She simply couldn't look him in the eye, he thought.

"I just don't know if it's a good idea," he went on.

"Really?" She picked up her untouched plate and stood, turning for the sink.

The frosty tone in her voice sent shards of ice plunging like daggers into his heart. He steeled himself against the pain beginning to well inside. His gaze shot to where she stood at the counter, her back, stiff as a board, to him.

Odd, how hard this was, when he'd been expecting it all along. He'd known all his life that he wasn't worth loving. And he'd known from the first day of this supposed marriage that it would soon end. And he would have been all right with that, if he hadn't allowed himself to care.

"The holiday itself or the idea of us celebrating it?" she asked, drawing him back from the dark thoughts circling his mind.

Anger churned in the pit of his stomach. But the fury was directed at himself, not her. This was his fault. He never should have slept with her. He never should have become accustomed to having her around. To her voice. Her scent. He never should have awakened himself to possibilities that he hadn't considered before.

Jack inhaled sharply, deeply, and said, "Let's stop kidding ourselves, all right?"

"Kidding ourselves?"

She still hadn't turned to look at him. Maybe it was better that way. If he looked into those deep brown eyes of hers, he might falter. Might back away from the only conclusion possible, "What happened between us last night was—"

"What?" She challenged, her fingers curling around the edge of the counter. "A mistake?"

He released a breath he hadn't realized he'd been holding. There. She'd said it. Surprising, really, how much it hurt to know that she, too, considered those few, magical hours to be an error in judgment.

"Donna." He tried to keep his voice steady, even, so she wouldn't know just how much this was costing him. "There's no reason to pretend that last night was anything more than a case of raging hormones. We're both adults. Sex is—"

"Don't say it," she snapped, suddenly turning on him, her dark brown eyes blazing with indignation.

"Say what?" Prepared for her regrets, her anger caught him off guard. Instinctively, he rose to face her.

"'Sex is no big deal, Donna,'" she said in a deep, false voice. Obviously doing an impression of someone who had once thrown those words at her, she went on. "'It has nothing to do with love. Don't be so naive.'"

"I didn't say that."

She jerked him a nod, then shoved her hair out of her eyes. "You didn't have to." Tossing her hands high, she let them fall to slap at her sides. "Amazing. How do I find you guys? What? Am I some kind of creep magnet?"

Donna stomped out of the room, and Jack was no more than two paces behind her. Blast her, he was doing the right thing. Something that was tearing him open inside. He'd be damned before he'd let her lump him in with some jerk without so much as an explanation.

He grabbed her arm, spinning her around to face him. "What the hell are you talking about?"

"You know exactly what I'm talking about." Her eyes seemed to sizzle with sparks of fury. She jerked out of his hold and faced him, chin up defiantly.

Whoever this jerk from her past was, he'd hurt her badly. Old pain was evident in her battle stance.

"Tell me," he said flatly.

"Four years ago, I was engaged to be married."

He nodded. He did remember something about a wedding that didn't happen.

"We were saving ourselves for marriage," she went on, snorting a choked laugh at her own stupidity. "We wanted making love together for the first time to be something...sacred."

He couldn't help feeling a twinge of disappointment. She had been willing to wait for sacred with a different man. With him, she'd given in to her desires. How was he supposed to take that?

"But two nights before the wedding," she continued, her voice strangled with remembered humiliation, "I found him with my maid of honor."

Anger rustled inside him. Anger for the hurt she'd suffered and because he hadn't been around to kick the man's ass for her.

She shook her head as if she still had a hard time believing it. "When I found them, he had the nerve to tell me that I was overreacting. That sex was no big deal and it didn't have a thing to do with his feelings for me."

"The bastard."

"Thank you," she said absently, and raced ahead. "I found out that he'd been *sacred* all over town." She started pacing wildly, her long, hurried steps carrying her back and forth across the tiny room in record time. "So I called off the wedding, made a fool of myself with my father's adjutant and then ran away.''

Huh? What was that last part? he wondered. Then he shrugged it off. Wasn't important at the moment. Besides, she was still talking, the words tumbling from her mouth in a rush, and if he didn't pay attention, he'd be lost.

"Gone four years," she was saying. "And the day I get back, I do it again. Only this time the man actually married me before he says sex doesn't mean anything." She threw a wild look at the ceiling and heaven beyond. "Is this some kind of weird cosmic joke?" she demanded. "Because if it is, I don't get it.''

"Donna," he interrupted, determined to at least defend himself against being lumped together with a lousy ex-fiancé.

"No, Jack. I don't want to hear it." She shot him a look that should have frozen him in his tracks. But marines were made of sterner stuff.

"I am not that bastard who cheated on you and hurt you," he shouted as she walked away from him, headed for their bedroom.

She paused in the doorway and glanced back at him. The ice in her eyes sent a chill through him that ran bone deep. And when she spoke, he knew it was over.

"No, Jack. You're the man who married me for my own good, *then* hurt me."

Twelve

For the next week, they moved like strangers through the little house. No, not strangers, Donna told herself. Strangers at least give each other the courtesy of polite nods and disinterested glances. She and Jack were more like ghosts. Neither of them even seeing the other.

Nights were the worst. Lying in the same bed, where the distance between them was measured like the legend on a map—inches equaled miles.

From her seat on the couch, Donna stared out the window at banks of massed gray clouds, rushing in to cover the sky with the threat of rain. November had arrived suddenly, as it often did in California. Cool, sunny days had disappeared into early morning fogs drifting in off the ocean and cold, damp winds.

She sighed and threw a quick glance at the kitchen timer sitting on the coffee table. One more minute and she'd know for sure. One more minute and her world would change dramatically. Her stomach pitched and rolled briefly and she took several deep breaths in a vain attempt to settle it.

When the timer chirped like a hysterical bird, she jumped and reached for it, stabbing the Off button with her fingertip. Silence crowded around her. She heard her own heartbeat thundering in her ears and imagined she could even hear another, fainter heartbeat marching in time with hers.

Slowly, she set the timer down and picked up the white plastic wand that held the answers to her immediate future. Hesitating only slightly, she looked down at the test squares.

A plus sign.

She gulped in a breath.

Her fingers closed tight around the wand. She felt the sharp sting of tears behind her eyes as she turned her head back to the window. Appropriately enough, the rain had started, splashing polka dots on the glass panes.

Donna wiped a tear from her cheek and blinked the rest of them back into submission. She wouldn't cry. She couldn't afford to. She had to be stronger than that. One hand dropped to her flat abdomen where her child was already growing, counting on her to keep it safe. And loved.

She knew what she had to do. Still clutching the

test stick, she stood and, to the accompanying patter of the rain, walked to her bedroom and started packing.

"You can't just leave," her father told her, "without so much as saying goodbye to the man."

"I can't say goodbye to Jack," Donna countered, and glanced at the closed door to her father's office before looking back at him. She knew damn well that if she tried to say goodbye, she'd never leave. And she had to go. For *all* their sakes.

"Donna," her father said, pushing himself out of his chair. Coming around the edge of the desk, he stopped directly in front of her and took both of her hands in his. "You're not thinking this through."

"Yes, I have," she told him, pulling free of him. If she gave in to the need for comfort now, she'd dissolve into a weeping, hysterical mess.

"What about the three months you agreed on?" he countered.

"Things have changed." To say the least.

"What things?"

She shook her head and blinked furiously, determined to keep the tears that were never far away, at bay awhile longer.

"You love him, Donna," he said softly, knowingly. "Even I can see that."

Pain tugged at her insides, poking, prodding.

"It doesn't matter."

"You're wrong," he said, and took the step that brought him right next to her. Laying both hands on her shoulders, he pulled her stiff form up against him and gave her a hug. "It's the only thing that *does* matter."

With his arms around her and her nose buried against his uniform blouse, Donna gave in briefly to the urge to be held. For most of her life her father had been there when she needed him. Ready to do battles on her behalf and right all the wrongs done to her.

She just wished he could fix this, too.

But he couldn't.

No one could.

"Daddy," she whispered, "you don't understand."

"I understand you're both being stubborn. And stupid."

She sniffed and confessed her secret. She had to tell *someone*. "I'm pregnant."

Taking her by the shoulders, he held her at arm's length, surprise etched on his features. "Are you sure?"

She nodded and silently cursed the solitary tear that had defied her to roll down her cheek.

"Does Jack know?"

"No," she said sharply and moved away from her father's gentle touch. "And he's not going to. Not for a while, anyway."

"You can't keep this from him, Donna," he said hotly. "A man has a right to know when he's going to be a father."

She knew all that. And she planned to tell him. In a few months maybe. Or after the baby was born.

Just not now. At the moment they both needed time and distance to recover from the charade of their marriage before they tried to work together as single parents.

"I plan to tell him," she countered. "Sometime soon. A month or two maybe. Not now."

"Why the hell not?" Tom Candello's voice lifted in outrage. He stared at her as if he'd never seen her before. "You're walking out on the bargain you two made *and* keeping the fact of his child from him? What's come over you, Donna?"

She snapped. "What's come over me?" she repeated, staring her father square in the eye. "Pride."

He snorted as if to brush away an insignificant factor.

"And it's about damn time, too," she went on, warming to her theme. "After Kyle made a fool of me, I didn't have much pride left."

He tried to interrupt, but she sailed on.

"Then, after I scared your assistant all the way to Greenland, I sank even lower. Heck, I couldn't even face *you* for four years and I *knew* you loved me."

"Donna—"

"Then I make a mess of things again, and Jack rides to the rescue." She threw her hands up in the air and shook her head. "He doesn't want to be married, Dad. He was protecting *your* reputation. He was trying to be a good guy. Hell, all he was missing was the white charger and shining armor."

"Donna, Jack knew what he was doing. No one forced him to marry you."

"No, you're right." She nodded and turned her back on him, walking to a window where she could stare out at Camp Pendleton as the heavens dumped at least an inch of rain on it. Outside, marines in foul-weather gear marched in formation and went about their daily duties despite the steady downpour. Because it *was* their duty. Honor demanded it. Pride.

Still looking at the rain, she continued, her tone softer, less strident now.

"The only thing that prodded Jack into marrying me was his own sense of honor."

"And that's bad?" her father asked, dumbfounded.

He didn't understand, and she wasn't sure she could explain it as clearly as she *felt* it. But, blast it, she knew she was right.

"Of course not," she said, and laid one hand on the cold, damp, rain-flecked windowpane. "His honor is part of who he is. It's so deeply ingrained in him, he never questions it and wouldn't be able to function without it."

"I don't see what you're getting at here," her father complained on a sigh.

She half turned to look at him. "Don't you get it, Dad? If Jack knew I was pregnant, he'd insist that we stay married. That we continue this charade that's only bringing both of us pain."

Tom Candello's features tightened.

"It's better this way," she assured him, trying not to sound as miserable as she felt. "I don't want a husband whose honor is the only thing keeping him with me.''

She waited what seemed like a lifetime but was probably no more than a few eternity-filled seconds.

At last, her father nodded in resignation. ''Where will you go?''

Donna wasn't sure if she was pleased or saddened that he had accepted the fact that her leaving was the right thing to do. Forcing a smile, she said, ''For the moment, back to Maryland. I can stay with my old roommate for a while. And I'm pretty sure I can get my old job back if I grovel appropriately.''

He gave her a wan smile, but nodded. ''When are you leaving?''

''Now.''

''Now?''

''I have a cab waiting outside,'' she told him. ''My flight out of San Diego is in two hours. I'll just wait at the airport.'' The truth of the matter was, that she hadn't been able to stay another minute in the tiny house where she'd known such intense joy and misery. She much preferred the sterile, impersonal lounge of a busy airport.

''So soon,'' he said, then held his arms out toward her. ''It feels like you've only been here a few minutes.''

She went to him, allowing herself to luxuriate in the comfort of his bear hug for several long minutes. ''I'm sorry I'll miss Thanksgiving dinner with you, but this way is better for me.''

He smoothed one hand over the back of her head. "I know, kiddo. I just wish you weren't leaving."

Donna pulled back from his embrace and lifted her chin. "I'll be okay, Daddy. Don't worry."

He laughed dryly. "Trust me. I'll worry. And not just about you. But about my grandchild, too." Then he shook his head as if he still couldn't believe it. "A grandfather. Amazing."

Donna reached out and patted his arm. "I have faith in you. You'll be a great grandpa."

"Long distance," he complained.

"Dad…"

He held up both hands in mock surrender.

She picked up her purse from the edge of his desk and started for the door. As she grabbed the doorknob, she turned to say, "I'll call you when I get in."

"Okay."

"And, Dad…" she said, her voice steely. "Don't say a word about the baby to Jack."

He looked offended. "May I remind you, young lady," he said, "that I am a full colonel in the United States Marine Corps? We are trained to keep secrets."

She wasn't convinced. "I mean it."

"Donna, it's up to you to tell him about the baby. But speaking as a man—and a father—don't wait too long."

Donna nodded stiffly and opened the door. An instant later she was gone.

Colonel Tom Candello waited an extra minute, to

make sure she was out of sight. Then he left his office to talk some sense into his son-in-law before it was too late.

The gray, rainy day perfectly complemented his mood, Jack thought grimly as he stared, unseeing, out the window. Even Tom had given up trying to talk to him and had run from the office, preferring Mother Nature's rainstorm to Jack's black frame of mind.

When his office door opened and closed again quickly, he didn't even turn to look at the interloper. "Whoever you are, turn around and get out."

"I'll pretend you didn't say that," the colonel said flatly.

Startled, Jack jumped to his feet, shooting his desk chair backward where it crashed into the wall and bounced off a gray steel file cabinet. "Colonel, Sir," he said. "My apologies. I didn't know it was you, Sir."

"At ease, Jack," the colonel told him. "I'm here as Donna's father, not your commanding officer."

Jack's stance relaxed, but he turned a wary eye on the man crossing the room to stand opposite his desk. "No offense, Colonel, but I don't have anything to say to my father-in-law."

"Good," the other man snapped, leaning both hands on the edges of the desk and pinning him with a sharp, dark brown gaze amazingly like his daughter's. "Then I'll talk. You listen."

"Sir—"

"Donna just left my office," the colonel went on.
Donna? Here? Just a few steps away?

"She had a cab waiting," the other man was saying.

"A cab?" Jack asked. "Why didn't she use the
truck?" He'd been riding to work with one of the
other sergeants so that Donna would have use of their
only vehicle.

"Because she's on her way to the airport."

He felt as though someone had just delivered a
solid blow to his midsection. Air left his lungs like
a balloon had been popped.

"The airport, Sir?" he repeated, surprised he was
able to speak at all past the sudden dryness in his
throat.

"She's leaving, Jack. For good."

Stunned, he said only, "Maybe that's for the best,
Sir." But inside, emotions tumbled through him,
leaving him shaken. He stiffened his legs in response,
to steady his stance. She hadn't even stayed the three
months they'd agreed on in the beginning.

How could he feel so empty and still be breathing?
he wondered. And how could his heart keep beating
when it was laying shattered in his chest?

"Not this time, Jack."

His gaze snapped to the older man's furious eyes.
"With all due respect, Sir," he said tightly, "this is
none of your business."

"Don't be a fool, Jack. Fight for your wife. Your
marriage."

"There's nothing to fight for," he muttered bleakly. "It's over."

"It's only over if you surrender or retreat," the colonel told him. "I've known you a long time, Jack, and I don't think I've seen you happier than you were with Donna. For a while, I thought it was going to work out."

So had he, Jack thought. In his dreams. His fantasies. It was only in reality that he lost her.

"If you *do* care for my daughter, fight for her," the colonel said, pushing up and away from the desk. "Don't make the same mistakes I did."

"Sir?"

"If I had been smarter," the colonel said, "I would have fought like hell to keep Donna's mother. If you love somebody enough, problems can be worked out."

"This isn't the same thing, Colonel," Jack said softly. "If Donna loved me or wanted to stay married, she wouldn't have left."

The colonel shook his head, clearly disgusted, then turned abruptly and stalked toward the door. He stopped and glanced back at Jack. "You tell yourself that, if it helps. And if I'm wrong and you don't love her, then stay here, First Sergeant, and let her go."

When he was alone again, Jack stared blankly at the closed door. Let her go? he thought, and felt a yawning emptiness open inside him. In his imagination, the years stretched out ahead of him. Long, lonely years that he would spend alone, wondering where Donna was and what she was doing. His nights would be filled with torturous images of Donna, lying in another man's arms, having another man's children.

His hands fisted tightly as that emptiness inside him blossomed, swelling into proportions large enough to swallow him whole. He stared into the blackness that was his life and realized the one fact that he'd been trying to deny for weeks. He loved her. *Really* loved her. So much so, that without her, his life would be an endless succession of barren days and desolate nights.

But she was gone. Left without a word.

Still, he asked himself, if he had admitted his love for her sooner, if he had risked rejection and confessed his feelings, would she have left?

He didn't know. But, damn it, he was through retreating. He was going to make a grab at the chance offered him. The chance for what so many lucky people took for granted every day. Love. Acceptance. Belonging to a family.

Moving quickly, he raced across the floor and out the door, then marched double-time to the colonel's office just down the hall. He knocked perfunctorily and pushed the door open wide enough to poke his head inside.

"Permission to take a personal day, Sir?" he asked.

"Granted," the colonel shouted to be heard over the already closing door. Then Tom Candello leaned back in his chair and grinned at the ceiling.

* * *

After checking in at the ticket window, Donna gripped the strap of her carry-on bag tighter and started walking across the terminal toward her gate. Other travelers, most of them in a much better frame of mind than she, pushed past her with muttered apologies, eager to be on their way. The weekday, afternoon crowd of people surprised her, but other than that, she paid little attention to any of them.

Weaving her way in and out of the mob of people and luggage, she hardly noticed when someone else bumped into her from behind. But when that someone made a grab for her tote bag, she turned around quickly and stopped dead.

"Jack?"

God, he looked wonderful. Soaking wet, his short hair plastered to his skull, rivulets of rain water coursing down his body to puddle on the shiny linoleum floor. He wiped one hand across his face irritably, then took her elbow in a firm, insistent grip.

"What are you doing?" she demanded as he started dragging her toward the exit.

"Taking you home," he said shortly, his voice carrying over the noise of the crowd and the squish-squeak of his combat boots on the floor.

Donna tossed a wild look around her, but no one was paying the slightest attention to her and the determined marine carrying her off. She could scream, she told herself, then immediately pictured the sensation that would cause.

Instead she planted her tennis shoes firmly in place and jerked herself free of him.

Grumbling quietly to himself, Jack only snatched her carry-on bag and started walking off again.

"Hey!" she shouted, and sprinted after him, finally getting a good grip on the strap of the bag and dragging him to a halt. "Give me my bag," she demanded.

He tugged at the strap, hauling her closer. "I'm not letting you go, Donna."

One brief, brilliant flash of hope rose up in her chest before fizzling out. For a moment she'd actually allowed herself to believe that he'd come for her because he loved her and couldn't lose her.

But there was a much bigger chance that her father had shot off his mouth, telling Jack about the baby.

She yanked on the cloth strap. "Go back to the base, Jack," she said, and was proud of herself for keeping her voice free of the emotion strangling her. "It's better this way. In a couple of months you can file for divorce and we can both go on with our lives."

Jack looked at her long and hard. How had he ever imagined that he would be able to live without her? All through that nightmare drive on a rain-slicked highway in a stolen—borrowed—Jeep, he'd rehearsed what he would say. Thought about how he should approach her.

Now that he was here, though, and faced with the most risky mission of his life, there was only one thing to do.

He let go of the bag and grabbed her in one smooth movement. Holding her tightly to his rain-soaked body, he coiled his arms around her. Her mouth opened in surprise and he lowered his head to take advantage of the possibilities.

The clamoring noise of the busy airport faded away. The bustling crowds of travelers dissolved into nothingness. His icy-cold, wet uniform held no discomfort anymore. There was only one reality in his universe and he was holding her.

Cupping the back of her head, he lay siege to her mouth, showing her without words that she was his breath, his heart…his life.

When at last he felt her go limp in his arms, he lifted his head, oblivious to the smiling faces of half the population of San Diego surrounding them.

Holding her face between his palms, his thumbs smoothed gently over her cheekbones and his gaze moved over her features hungrily. Then he said the words he'd thought he would never have the opportunity to say. "I love you."

She blinked and a solitary tear trickled from the corner of her eye. His right thumb caught it and wiped it away. He would spend the rest of his life seeing to it that she never had a reason to cry again.

As resolve filled him, he said the words again. "I *love* you, Donna." When she still didn't speak, he fought a frisson of panic and continued in his best, no-nonsense voice. "And you'd damn well better love me back. That's an order."

A long moment ticked by before she grinned. "Yes, First Sergeant," she snapped before throwing herself into his arms.

His heart started beating again as he buried his face in the crook of her neck, inhaling the sweetness of her perfume and reveling in the warmth of her love.

Then he reached down, grabbed up her bag and tossed the strap over his shoulder. When that was done, he swept her up into his arms and smiled like a idiot when she wrapped her arms around his neck.

And to the sounds of applause and hoots of approval from the crowd, he carried her back to the Jeep—and home.

As the rain pelted against the windows and the quiet gray light of a stormy afternoon filled their tiny bedroom, they lay exhausted in each other's arms.

"I love you," Jack whispered, and bent to trail a line of kisses down her throat.

"I love you." Donna sighed and tipped her head to one side, allowing him easier access. Her fingertips smoothed across his shoulders and she smiled, more happy than any one woman had a right to be.

Propping himself up on one elbow, Jack looked down at her, suddenly serious. As his right hand skimmed along her body, creating a ribbon of gooseflesh in its wake, he said, "I never thought that I would be saying those words to anyone."

She smiled up at him. "Get used to them, I'll want to hear them often."

"I love you," he whispered, and bent his head to kiss her. "You are everything I always wanted and never counted on having."

"Oh, Jack..." Tears stung the backs of her eyes, but she refused to cry. Not on the happiest day of her life.

He leaned over and planted a quick, hard kiss on her tummy. "I hope we just made a baby, Donna. I want to have children with you."

Her breath caught in her throat and those darn tears filled her eyes again.

He kissed her, a soft, swift kiss, then went on. "I want to build a family with you, Donna. The family I always wanted but never thought I'd find."

She reached up and dusted her palm along the side of his face. How could she ever have even considered leaving this strong, gentle man? she wondered, and then smiled at him proudly.

"You want babies?" she asked. "Well, Marine, this is your lucky day. Have I got a surprise for you."

* * * * *

Take 2 bestselling love stories FREE

Plus get a FREE surprise gift!

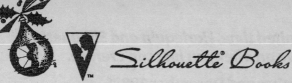

For a limited time, Harlequin and Silhouette have an offer you just can't refuse.

In November and December 1998:

BUY **ANY** TWO HARLEQUIN OR SILHOUETTE BOOKS and
SAVE $10.00
off future purchases

OR BUY ANY THREE HARLEQUIN OR SILHOUETTE BOOKS AND **SAVE $20.00** OFF FUTURE PURCHASES!

(each coupon is good for $1.00 off the purchase of two
Harlequin or Silhouette books)

JUST BUY 2 HARLEQUIN OR SILHOUETTE BOOKS, SEND US YOUR NAME, ADDRESS AND 2 PROOFS OF PURCHASE (CASH REGISTER RECEIPTS) AND HARLEQUIN WILL SEND YOU A COUPON BOOKLET WORTH **$10.00** OFF FUTURE PURCHASES OF HARLEQUIN OR SILHOUETTE BOOKS IN 1999. SEND US 3 PROOFS OF PURCHASE AND WE WILL SEND YOU 2 COUPON BOOKLETS WITH A TOTAL SAVING OF **$20.00**. (ALLOW 4-6 WEEKS DELIVERY) OFFER EXPIRES DECEMBER 31, 1998.

I accept your offer! Please send me a coupon booklet(s), to:

NAME: _____

ADDRESS: _____

CITY: _____ STATE/PROV.: _____ POSTAL/ZIP CODE: _____

Send your name and address, along with your cash register receipts for proofs of purchase, to:

In the U.S.	In Canada
Harlequin Books	**Harlequin Books**
P.O. Box 9057	P.O. Box 622
Buffalo, NY	Fort Erie, Ontario
14269	L2A 5X3

PHQ4982

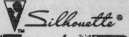

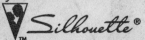

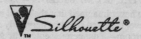

SILHOUETTE® Desire®

COMING NEXT MONTH